When Jason came to the house later that afternoon, she was waiting for him at the door.

"Something's going on, and I want to know what it is," she told him, stepping aside so he could enter.

"What kind of something?" he asked.

"Every time I have a guest, something embarrassing happens to him. I want to know why."

His head came up a fraction, his jaw clamped tight, and a little pink showed around his ears. "That would be hard to say, Sharon," he said slowly.

"Not hard to say. Hard to admit." She faced him square on, a determined glint in her eyes.

His expression changed, and he stepped closer. "A girl who's had so much schooling should have all the answers, don't you think? Open your eyes, Sharon. You are a wealthy woman. What exactly do you think has been going on? Do you think those Romeos never thought about getting their hands on the Lazy H?"

He moved so close that she could see the tiny brown mole beside his mouth. His gaze burned into hers. "Which would you rather have, an opportunist who wants to use you to get what Rudolph worked so hard to build, or someone who cares for you because you're sweet, and spunky, and smart?"

ROSEY DOW

Winner of the coveted Christy Award for *Reaping the Whirlwind*, Rosey Dow is a bestselling author with a dozen published novels. A popular conference speaker and writing workshop presenter, Rosey has been a guest on dozens of radio programs and directs www. christianfictionmentors.com. Visit her Web site at www.roseydow.com.

Books by Rosey Dow

HEARTSONG PRESENTS

Don't miss out on any of our super romances. Write to us at the following address for information on our newest releases and club information.

Heartsong Presents Readers' Service
PO Box 721
Uhrichsville, OH 44683

Or visit www.heartsongpresents.com

Sharon Takes a Hand

Rosey Dow

Heartsong Presents

To Jeanne Dow, my proofreader extraordinaire, my kind mother-in-law, and my dear friend. I love you!

A note from the Author:
I love to hear from my readers! You may correspond with me by writing:

Rosey Dow
Author Relations
PO Box 721
Uhrichsville, OH 44683

ISBN 978-1-59789-624-5

SHARON TAKES A HAND

Our mission is to publish and distribute inspirational products offering exceptional value and biblical encouragement to the masses.

PRINTED IN THE U.S.A.

one

June 4, 1891

Sharon Hastings shifted an eighth of an inch on the unforgiving leather seat of the dusty stagecoach. For more than an hour, the rotund lady next to her had been droning on about her marvelous grandchildren. Sharon made some kind of reply from time to time, but the woman's voice had faded into a jumble of sounds. The only thing on Sharon's mind today was a single word. It rang and rumbled through her thoughts with steady intensity—a chant, a sonnet, a song: *home.*

More than a thousand nights she'd closed her eyes and pressed her cheek into her boarding school pillow, holding that word close to her heart. She'd spent five years studying the three R's, perfecting her form on the violin, and faithfully adhering to Mrs. Minniver's Rules of Decorum. Headmistress at the school of fifty girls, Mrs. Minniver was a kind of sword-wielding archangel—perfectly groomed, precise, and terrifying.

Two weeks before, Sharon had received tickets for the train and for the stage from her guardian, Rudolph Hastings, with a one-sentence note saying he'd pick her up at the station in Farmington, New Mexico. She'd arrive a week after her eighteenth birthday.

When she was thirteen years old, Sharon's parents and sister had succumbed to cholera while traveling on the Oregon Trail. Soon afterward, her father's brother, Rudolph, had arranged for her boarding school. He'd sent her presents at all the right times and given her a generous allowance for clothes, but he never came to Springfield, Missouri, to see her. She'd never been to the Lazy H ranch. She'd never once met her benefactor.

When she'd sent a letter asking him if she could visit the ranch, he had responded by saying the Lazy H was no place for a young girl like her. She'd had to be content to spend her holidays with her best friend, Candace Matthews, and a dozen other girls who also didn't leave the school for holidays.

Today, none of that mattered. Today, she was coming home.

When the stage reached Farmington, Sharon was the last to disembark. Her trunks were already on the boardwalk when she stepped down. From an old tintype photograph, she knew that Uncle Rudolph looked a lot like her father except shorter. She should be able to recognize him.

The boardwalk creaked under the weight of a dozen people and at least that many trunks. Everyone was chattering, hugging, and gathering their belongings. Everyone except Sharon.

Several minutes passed, and no one had stepped forward to speak to her. Careful to maintain her poise (Rule 1 on Mrs. Minniver's List), she commanded her hands to stop fidgeting with the folds of her gray twill skirt (Rule 2).

For five long years she'd lived by the decalogue of the headmistress and could recite each of its strictures forward and backward:

1. Maintain your poise at all times.

2. Never touch your person or adjust your clothes in public. Fidgeting is forbidden.

3. Always keep the voice modulated and gentle.

4. When in polite company, engage in intelligent conversation. Seek to find common interests that both parties will enjoy.

5. When asked how you are or any polite question that doesn't require a complete answer, say, "Fine," and thank the speaker for asking.

6. Always say thank you for even the smallest kindness.

7. Sit with the spine away from the chair back, with hands folded and ankles crossed.

8. Never laugh aloud in public.

9. When outdoors, always keep your head covered.

10. Always maintain a calm and sedate pace. Never dash about.

❧

The street was hard-packed brown earth. A double row of false-fronted shops stretched out as far as she could see in both directions. Someone nearby was cooking cabbage seasoned with salt pork.

"Miss Hastings?" a deep voice asked from behind her.

She turned to see a giant, dark-haired cowboy—complete with chaps and a cowhide vest. He had a boyish face with a thick jaw and eyes the color of brushed steel. He held a brown Stetson against the side of his leg. Beside him stood a slim, hatless man wearing a blue pinstripe suit, his black hair slicked back from a center part.

"Yes, and you are. . . ?"

The cowboy spoke. His voice was hard and dry. "I'm Jason

Riordan, foreman at the Lazy H. This is Edward Kellerman, Rudolph's lawyer."

The attorney smiled into her eyes and made a tiny formal bow. She offered him her gloved hand. "How do you do, gentlemen?" she asked. As an afterthought, she shook hands with the cowboy.

"Where's my uncle?" she asked, looking behind them.

"Miss Hastings," Kellerman said, "would you mind stepping into my office?" His words were precise with no trace of a Western drawl. "We need to speak to you about some private matters. It's only a few steps from here."

She gazed at her trunks piled on the boardwalk.

The foreman said, "I'll have my men load your things on the wagon. A couple of the boys came to town to fetch some oats and cracked corn. They're heading back now." He gave a signal to a lean cowboy who looked as thin and tough as a strip of dried leather.

"What's this about?" she asked, falling in step with the men.

Kellerman's squarish face lit up as he smiled. "How was your trip?"

"It was fine, Mr. Kellerman," she said, remembering Rule 5. "Thank you for asking." Actually, the trip was hot, confining, and—worst of all—intensely boring.

Leaving the stage station behind, they passed a one-story building that called itself a hotel. Next was the Farmington General Store. Wearing black garters over his white shirt-sleeves, a young blond man came out, glanced at Sharon, and nodded before hurrying down the street in the opposite direction.

The cowboy's boots clomped on the boardwalk. He greeted a passing older woman with a brief, "Miss," and a tug on his hat brim.

Edward Kellerman's office was next, a single room over

a milliner's shop. Holding her skirts up to clear her feet, Sharon climbed stairs so narrow that her elbows sometimes bumped either wall.

A heavy desk, a bookcase, and two chairs filled Kellerman's office. The room smelled like linseed oil and old leather with a hint of sweet pipe-tobacco smoke clinging to the air. Sharon sat down as Mr. Kellerman moved to his seat behind the desk. The foreman stood near the door.

Taking in the somber expressions of both men, Sharon's throat tightened. "Where is Uncle Rudolph?" she asked again.

"Miss Hastings," Edward Kellerman said, "your uncle had an accident. He went missing six weeks ago."

Sharon's breath left her. Where would she go? Her only other relative was her mother's sister, a widow with eight children to feed.

The lawyer reached into a drawer and removed a long sheaf of papers. "At this point, we all agree that if Rudolph Hastings were living, he would have come home by now."

The foreman cleared his throat. "We've searched and searched until every one of us gave out. Rudolph knew his land so well that if he could, he would have found a way to make himself known to us when we were passing by him." He rubbed his jaw with his calloused fingers. "He must have fallen into a ravine or. . ." He hesitated and glanced at Sharon. "There's wildcats and bears out there, Miss Hastings."

Sharon shivered.

Mr. Kellerman went on, "I have here your uncle's will, Miss Hastings. I know this is a shock to you, but I have to tell you that he left almost everything he owned to you—the ranch, the cattle, everything."

She pulled a handkerchief from the pocket of her gray traveling jacket and touched her nose with it. "Mr. Kellerman," she whispered, "I need a moment to take this in."

He stood. "Certainly. I'll fetch you a glass of water." He hurried out.

Sharon closed her eyes and her head spun. Her breath came in short, shallow gasps.

Mr. Kellerman returned and pressed a glass into her hands. "Here. Sip this. You'll feel better."

"Thank you," she murmured, then drank the cool liquid.

Foreman Riordan spoke from behind her. She had forgotten he was there. His words were friendly, but his voice was strained. "Would you like to stay in town tonight? I can bunk at the livery stable if you want to get a hotel room."

Still trying to regain control, she turned to him. "That won't be necessary, Mr. Riordan."

She handed the glass to Kellerman. "Thank you. That did help." She drew in a slow breath to continue calming herself. "Do you need anything else from me, Mr. Kellerman?"

"Edward," he said, smiling. "At your service." He gave that small bow again. "And no, there is nothing else. If I need you to sign any papers, I'll ride out to the ranch. It isn't so far."

The cowboy said, "An hour on horseback, twice that in the surrey."

"Did you say a surrey?" Sharon asked, turning toward him in surprise.

"Yes, Miss Hastings. Rudolph took real pride in that surrey. He ordered it brought in from Abilene two years ago. Corky keeps it blacked up and polished, so it still looks brand-new. I thought it would be more fittin' for a lady than the buckboard."

An hour later, Jason helped Sharon into the surrey, and they set off. With its flat roof and fringe swaying all around the top, Sharon felt like she was riding in high style. It was a perfect June day. A light breeze carried the faint aroma of sage and cedar. So many thoughts and feelings coursed through Sharon's brain, she felt as if her bonnet were shrinking against her scalp.

The land was rugged and dry, dotted with scrub brush and bits of grass that seemed to stretch to infinity. A gentle breeze cooled her forehead and slowly, gradually settled her mind. For the first time in her life, she had options. She could sell the ranch or stay on and live here. But nothing had to be decided today.

She let out a slow breath and began to relax.

Jason Riordan kept his eyes straight ahead. After a while Sharon began to search her brain for some statement to start a polite conversation (Rule 4). Oh, what could she say? Why didn't *he* say something?

Finally, she blurted, "What's the ranch like?"

He glanced at her.

Was that a surprised expression on his face? Her voice had sounded awfully loud when she'd asked that. Had she broken Rule 3? If only willpower could force her cheeks to cool. The new owner of the Lazy H shouldn't be blushing like a schoolgirl, even if she was one.

Gazing at a spot over the horse's head, he said, "The Lazy H covers two thousand acres, give or take a few hundred. We run steers and horses, and we have the biggest water hole for miles around. The homestead has a bunkhouse, a corral and barn, and Rudolph's house, of course."

"Please, tell me what happened to Uncle Rudolph," she said. "What kind of accident did he have?"

His expression grew troubled. "We don't know what happened, miss. He went out riding one morning and never came back. His horse came in with an empty saddle shortly before dark. There was a lot of blood on it." He rubbed his jaw. "We've all been tore up about it. Can't seem to get settled down."

"Perhaps someone just kidnapped him? Indians or outlaws?"

He started and sent her a disbelieving look. "We don't have Indian trouble hereabouts. And even if we did, what would Indians want with an old sidewinder like Rudolph? He'd be too dangerous for them to keep alive—for anyone to keep alive."

He paused a moment, then went on. "We searched for days from dawn to dark, and never came up with a single track or scrap of cloth or anything to help us. He started out riding for the water hole, but who knows where he went after that. Could have been anywhere, on our land or off it." He took off his hat and wrapped his arm around his forehead to blot the perspiration with his sleeve.

Replacing his Stetson, he said, "It's a puzzle. There are some broken hills north of here where he could have fallen into a ravine, but I can't see Rudolph being so foolish as to get that close to the edge. He'd lived here for years. He knew every square foot of the place."

He leaned forward with his elbows resting on his thighs, both hands gripping the reins. His jaw had the barest hint of a five o'clock shadow.

"Do you think there could have been foul play? Did he have any enemies?"

"Everyone has enemies, Miss Hastings. Rudolph had his share. There were a couple of old grudges and the like, but were they big enough to cause someone to do away with him?" He shook his head. "Nah. If someone was that fiery mad, they'd call him out and try out a fast draw. This is New Mexico, not New York."

Sharon let that seep into her brain for a few minutes. There had to be a plausible reason that Rudolph had disappeared without a trace. Unfortunately, she knew too little about the life here to make any more guesses.

Finally, she said, "Those mountains are beautiful. What are they called?"

"That's the tail end of the Rockies, the Sangre de Cristos. That mountain there," he pointed northeast, "is Taos. It's about ten thousand feet high, from what I understand. Farther south is Santa Fe Mountain. That one goes up to twelve thousand feet."

"Have you ever climbed them?"

He shot her a disbelieving look. "Why would I want to do that? Mountain climbing is for tourists. Out here folks ride most everywhere they go."

She rushed on. "The train came through a long, winding gorge. Those must be the same mountains that we came through." She smiled shyly. "We studied the Rocky Mountains in geography, of course. I can tell you all about them, but I've never lived near them like this." She went on wistfully, "My folks and my little sister died in the Colorado foothills. We never even made it to the first mountain."

He shifted to a more upright position on the seat and glanced in her general direction. "I'm sorry," he said, his voice softening a little. "That must have been real tough."

She didn't know what to say in reply to that, so she let some time pass.

Finally, she asked, "How many hired hands do you have?"

"Two full-timers, besides me and Max, the cook. We'll hire more for roundup." He gave her an edgy look. "Miss Hastings, I can run the ranch for you. I've lived here all my life, and my father was foreman right up until he died."

"I have no doubt that you are capable, Mr. Riordan," she said, moistening her lips. "I'd very much appreciate your help. As you know, I'm at a distinct disadvantage."

He turned to look her full in the face. "You sure did get a sight of book learning at that school, didn't you?"

"What do you mean?" she asked, wondering if she should be offended.

"Miss, you won't get too far with the hands, talking like

that. We're plain-speaking folks hereabouts."

Her chin came up a fraction of an inch. "Well, so am I."

He stiffened. Looking away, he ran his thumb and forefinger down either side of his mouth, then looked at her again. "Yes, miss."

"Would you do me a great favor?"

"Of course."

"Don't call me *miss* anymore. I don't like it. Please call me Sharon."

He touched the brim of his hat and nodded. "We don't *mister* much out here, so you can call me Jason." He reached under the seat and picked up a small box. "Here. Open this. It's our supper. Max will have finished putting the food away before we get there, so I picked this up at the hotel restaurant."

The smell of fried chicken was heavenly. Fresh-baked rolls and thick-cut fried potatoes. She was starving.

She poked around inside the pasteboard container. No plates or silverware or napkins. Jason pulled off his gloves and picked up a crusty chicken leg.

Intent on supper, she carefully removed her white cotton gloves and placed them in her handbag. Before long, she was munching chicken and licking her salty fingers, remembering younger days and wishing she could taste her mother's cooking one more time.

At least the food kept them busy for a while. Trying to hold polite conversation with this man was exhausting.

two

They rode into the ranch at the edge of dark. Though still fully visible, the yard had shadowy corners. The greens and browns glowed rich and deep, and the scent of horses and straw hung in the air. The lane split into a Y shape, the wide right side heading for the barn and a long, low building beyond it. The narrow left side led to the house. That part of the lane stretched out beside the porch, then circled a giant tree and rejoined the stem of the Y.

A short man a few years past middle age stood on the porch. He had a large face and a round body. His head was completely bald, and he wore a white apron that almost touched the floor.

"Max!" Jason called, a humorous note in his voice. "Meet Miss Hastings—Sharon." He turned to Sharon. "Your cook, Max Martin. He'll take good care of you."

Max bounded down the stairs and helped her from the surrey. "Miss Hastings! It's so good to meet you!"

When she stepped to the ground, she was at least four inches taller than he was. She shook his hand. "It's nice to meet you, Mister Mart—"

"Max!" he said. "Just Max." He turned to Jason still in the surrey. "Wilson brought her trunks from town. We put them in the master bedroom."

Jason nodded. "You having hotcakes for breakfast?" he asked.

"Beef and biscuits, but if you want hotcakes, I'll make hotcakes."

"Another day," Jason said, grinning as he shook the reins.

"Thank you, Jason!" she called to him as the surrey began to move, remembering Rule 6 just in time.

"My pleasure." Without looking directly at her, he touched the brim of his Stetson and set off. The wheels of the surrey made grating sounds on the driveway as he rounded the sharp curve.

"This way, Sharon," Max said, beaming up at her. "I'll show you your room." As he opened the door, he went on, "Rudolph couldn't wait for the day when you'd come." He sobered. "I only wish he was here to welcome you like he dreamed of doing." He stepped aside for her to enter.

In the center of the open room stood a massive stone fireplace with a wide hearth. A long-barreled shotgun hung over it. The fireplace stones were round, smooth, river rock in varying shades of yellow and orange. The hearth stones were flat and gray. Two matching camelback sofas closely flanked the fireplace with two rocking chairs at the outside end. The floor was made of dark planks in various widths with deep cracks between some of them.

Max led her toward the right. "Your room is in the back," he said. "The two doors off the living room lead to the other bedrooms. We have three bedrooms in all. Rudolph built this house for a family, but he never married." He chuckled sadly. "We were both bachelors, he and I. We used to play checkers in the evenings." He shook his head. "I'm sure glad to see you come, Miss Sharon. This place has been like a tomb since he's been gone."

The kitchen filled the entire back half of the house, and Sharon was surprised to see another fireplace, back-to-back with the first one. This one had no hearth, and the firebox was taller and deeper. It had iron pothooks on both sides of the blackened opening.

"That's the old cooking setup," Max said. "Now I have a

woodstove with a hot water reservoir." He proudly pointed to the black porcelain Enterprise cookstove on the opposite wall. "We have an inside pitcher pump, too." A red water pump sat on the counter near the back door, its long handle extending well below the edge of the counter for better leverage.

He turned to the bedroom door that opened from the kitchen. "This was your uncle's room, and now it's yours. I left everything mostly as he had it." He led the way inside. "I took out his clothes and put them in one of the spare rooms. You can decide what to do with them later."

Sharon slowly stepped across the threshold. A giant bed dominated the room. It had massive round posts at each corner and was covered with a faded Texas star quilt. A small fireplace faced the end of the bed. Her trunks stood in a row before the fireplace.

"I put water in the pitcher on the dry sink," Max said, stepping back through the door. "If you want anything, I'll be around for another half hour. I'm setting up some sourdough." He reached for the door latch. "I bunk with the hands. If you need me, jangle the triangle on the front porch and I'll come a-running."

"Thank you, Max. I'm sure I'll be fine. Good night." She reached for her bonnet strings.

Twenty minutes later, her traveling gown lay draped over her trunks, and she slipped into a cotton gown. It was barely past dark, but she was exhausted.

The bed was soft. The night was cool. Sinking deep into the feather pillow, Sharon let out a long, weary sigh. She felt like she'd been holding her breath for five years. Closing her eyes, she fell into a deep, dreamless sleep.

&

When Sharon opened her eyes, a faint gray light came through the room's four windows. She heard pans clanking in the kitchen and gruff voices speaking low. Throwing off the quilt, she padded to the pitcher and basin on the stand. The morning was pleasantly cool. The air felt thin. It was a welcome relief after the humidity in Missouri.

She came from her room, wearing a wrinkled housedress that she'd found lying near the top in one of her trunks. Shaking and smoothing the fabric had hardly loosened the deep-set creases.

Max stood at the dishpan next to the pitcher pump. "Well, Miss Sharon!" he exclaimed. Drying his hands on his apron, he lifted a clean plate from the stack beside him. "I saved you a steak and some biscuits." He forked them onto the plate. "Care for some milk? I can fetch some from the springhouse."

"That's not necessary," she said. "Do you have any coffee left?"

He chuckled. "We have coffee all day long. It's ranch house tradition." He set her plate on the table.

"I was hoping to meet the hands this morning," she said, looking across the long, bare table beside her. She pulled out the head chair and sat well away from its back.

"We serve breakfast at five o'clock," Max replied, filling two enamel cups with coffee. "The hands are usually on the range by six." He sat down near her.

"Six?" She picked up her fork. There were no napkins in sight, and she was too uncomfortable to ask for one. "I'll have to get up earlier. Would you mind knocking on my door when you come in to make breakfast?"

"At four o'clock in the morning?" he asked, surprised.

"I'd appreciate it, Max." She sipped the coffee. It was strong. "This whole situation makes me feel strange, like I'm walking around in a Dickens novel instead of real life. I came here expecting to meet my uncle. I was so looking forward to getting to know him. And now..."

Max nodded. "You're not the only one. We've all been

wandering around here like lost boys. Even though we know that Rudolph's not coming back, we still keep waiting. That's the only way I can explain it. We're all still waiting. I wonder if we'll ever stop."

"I wanted to thank him," Sharon said. "For five long years, I've been waiting to thank him in person." She sipped her coffee.

He smiled with his lips and also with his eyes. "The best thanks you could ever give him is to take care of the ranch for him. He loved this place like most men love their wives. It was his whole life."

Setting down her coffee cup, she met his gaze. "That's exactly what I'm going to do." Her chin came up. "And one more thing, if someone hurt Uncle Rudolph, I'm going to find out about that, too."

He grinned. "Your teachers' reports showed you have spunk. Rudolph read them to me, and we chuckled over 'em." He leaned in. "If you need anything, anything at all, call me and I'll come running."

From the head of the table, she could see into the far right section of the living room. The morning light revealed the dusty corners and the grimy windows.

Max turned to follow her line of sight. "I'm a cook, Miss Sharon, not a housekeeper. Mrs. Riordan used to come in to clean for Rudolph, but she's got arthritis. It got worse last Christmas, and she had to quit. He never got anyone else."

"The foreman's wife?" she asked.

"His mother," Max said. "His pa used to be foreman, and his ma worked in the house up until five years ago when she took sick. That's when I came to cook for him. After that, she came in once a week to clean. About six months ago she had to give that up, too." He shook his head regretfully. "Wonderful woman, Agnes Riordan. It's such a shame."

"Don't worry about the cleaning," Sharon told him, turning her attention to breakfast. "I grew up on a farm in Missouri until I was twelve. I can ride, plant, sew, scrub clothes, and clean. My father got the itch to go west, and that's how my parents and sister caught cholera. I didn't get to boarding school until I was thirteen." She smiled wryly. "I was gangly as a newborn colt when I got there. And I could never keep my hair out of my eyes."

She felt his gaze upon her perfectly coiled blond French twist and stifled the urge to run her hand across it. Poor Miss Rollings, her personal dresser, had worked with her for almost a year before Sharon could manage her hip-length tresses alone.

"What happened to Uncle Rudolph, Max?" she asked, moving the subject away from herself. "What do you think?"

His face darkened. "I haven't the first notion what happened to him. He was canny in the saddle, an old veteran. He'd raised his horse, Star, from a colt, had him for about fifteen years, and rode him almost every day. I can't see Star throwing Rudolph off, or even leaving him if he was hurt. But he did." He tapped his fingers on the table. "None of it makes a lick of sense."

They were silent for a moment, then Max said, "Rudolph used to joke about his Cattleman's Treasure when he was jawing with a group of men. He wouldn't say what it was, and that got some men riled."

"What was it?"

He sipped his coffee. "He never told anyone. That's the frustrating thing. Now, we may never know."

"Could it have been gold or silver, do you think?"

Max set down his cup. "If it was, he would have never admitted it. Remember what happened to poor Sutter in California? He lost everything."

A few minutes later, she set down her fork. "I'm sorry. It's delicious, but I can't finish it all."

He chuckled. "I'm used to feeding big cowboys, miss," he said. "Don't you worry about it." He stood and picked up her plate. "I'd best get started on lunch. I'm going to chip up the beef left from breakfast and make a thick stew."

Sharon took a last sip of coffee and set her cup on top of the enamel plate. "Thank you, Max." She smiled. "That was wonderful."

"You're welcome, miss."

"Sharon," she said, standing. "I'd rather you call me Sharon."

He grinned, showing her a row of thick teeth, then hurried back to his dishpan.

She returned to her room to start the tiresome job of unpacking. The bedroom contained a highboy with six drawers and a small chest with four. On the wall next to the door stood a narrow wardrobe with three more drawers and a fifteen-inch space for hanging clothes. Five pegs behind the door held two old hats and a worn leather gun belt holding a gleaming revolver.

She asked Max where she could find a mop, a broom, and some old rags, then began by giving the entire bedroom a good cleaning. By the time she was finished, the room was filled with light from its four sparkling windows. She threw them all open and let the wispy breeze clear out the last hint of dusty smell. She even swept out the fireplace.

Getting her things out of their trunks was another matter altogether. Uncle Rudolph had been very generous with her clothing allowance. Maybe too generous. She filled the drawers and then jammed her eight dresses and four crinolines into the wardrobe. The massive skirts competed for space and bulged out the front. This was an ironing disaster. Everything in there would stay constantly wrinkled.

Finally, she went back through everything to sort out what she really needed. Where was she going to wear all of this now? When Max jangled the triangle, calling for lunch, she had five gowns lying in a mound on the quilt. She dabbed at her hair with a brush to smooth the stray wisps before she went out. Closing the bedroom door carefully behind her, she joined the men.

Two of the hands were already seated at the table, but they immediately stood when she entered the room. Conversation died.

"Men, meet Miss Sharon Hastings," Jason Riordan said. He held the head chair for her, and she sat down.

Max stepped up, a large pot of stew in his hands. "She's been up since before six," he announced, as though he were proud.

Sharon felt like a prize calf at the county fair. "Please be seated," she said, trying to smile. Her heart was jumping in her throat. "I don't want you to stand on ceremony on my behalf."

"Let's get the names out of the way," Jason said. "This is Corky McCormick and his two boys, Roddy and Mike." The boys were in their early teens, she guessed. They both had dark auburn hair like their father. "They live on the back side of the range. Their third boy, Ian, had to stay at home and help his ma today." Roddy grinned at Sharon. Mike stared at the floor. Somewhere between thirty and forty years old, Corky was of medium height with craggy cheeks and dark, intense eyes. He had a deep crease going up from the bridge of his nose into his forehead.

"Howdy, miss," he said. When he shook Sharon's hand, his palm felt stiff.

Jason held out his hand toward the second cowboy who was taller and leaner than Corky. He was the same one who had brought her trunks home from town. "Wilson Gants," Jason said. "He lives in the bunkhouse with me and Max." Wilson's face was scrawny. He had thinning brown hair and a deep scar that showed through the thick stubble on his right cheek.

"Miss," he said, ducking his head. Quickly, he pressed her hand and glanced at her. He stepped back, then shied away from looking at her again.

The plank table was set for eight with blue enamel plates and coffee mugs, some tin and some enamel. Chairs scraped across the plank floor as they all took their places. The stew smelled meaty and rich.

"Jason," Sharon said, "would you offer thanks for the food?"

He didn't say anything in reply but bowed his head and offered a blessing over the food. His words were smooth and natural sounding, like he was used to saying them.

While they ate, Jason asked, "Will you need anything from me today?"

She set down her spoon. "Not today, Jason. Would you mind showing me over the range tomorrow?"

He hesitated. "You may have forgotten that tomorrow is Sunday," he said.

"Oh, that's right. I'm sorry. I'm all confused from so many days of traveling. Do you attend worship?"

He nodded. "My mother, my sister, and I are members of the Farmington Congregational Church. In weather like this, we usually take a buckboard to town. Too many people for the surrey."

"What time do you leave?"

"I usually leave here at seven o'clock," he said. "I stop by the cabin to fetch Ma and my sister, Lucy. Corky's family comes along."

"Would you mind if I join you?"

He grinned. "Not at all. My sister, Lucy, will be glad to meet you."

"I'm looking forward to meeting her and your mother, too," she said.

"On Monday, we can ride over the ranch if you'd like." His brow twisted and he stammered, "We—don't have a sidesaddle, miss—I mean, Sharon."

She let out a soft laugh. "I can ride, Jason, and I don't need a sidesaddle to do it."

She looked up to see six pairs of male eyes on her. Her cheeks felt like they were on fire. Swallowing a sip of coffee, she went on a bit louder. "So I won't have to repeat this over and over again, I want to tell you all a little about myself and what my plans are at the moment." She gazed at each man in turn. Wilson Gants and young Mike McCormick focused on their empty plates.

She told them where she grew up, then how she came to be an orphan and a ward of Uncle Rudolph. "This has been a shock to all of us, and I'm going to need your help for the next few weeks while I get my mind settled. You're all concerned with the future of the ranch and how my being here is going to affect things. I want to be very fair to all of you. I need some time to sort things out."

Picking up her spoon, Sharon paused. "I do have one request," she said. "Please don't call me *miss* or *ma'am*. While I was at school, we had to call everyone *miss* or *ma'am*—the teachers, the dorm mothers, the aides, and the cleaning ladies. I came to despise the terms. My name is Sharon, and I'd appreciate it if you'd address me that way."

Roddy nudged Mike, and the boys shared a secret smile.

Sharon noticed the move. Jason leaned toward her to whisper, "They think you talk funny. That's what they're grinning about."

"I suppose I must," she murmured. "As I recall, you think so, too."

His lips twitched. The next moment, he turned to speak to Corky on his other side.

≈

On Sunday morning, the breakfast hour was moved back to six o'clock, but Sharon was out of bed well before then.

Wearing a dress of burgundy silk and white lace with a matching hat and parasol, Sharon stepped outside as Jason said, "Whoa," and pulled back on the reins to stop the wagon beside the porch. He wore a black suit with a black felt hat, a great change from his cowboy garb. The two-seater buckboard had wool blankets draped over both seats.

The instant Jason caught sight of her, his expression changed. That instant Sharon knew she had overdressed for the occasion. Why hadn't she worn the dark blue calico? At school, that would have been considered a day dress, but here it would have been perfect for Sunday meeting.

It was too late now. She'd spent more than an hour coaxing the wrinkles from this gown. The calico dress hung limply from a peg, still waiting for her attention.

Jason jumped down and came around to help her up. "Good morning," he said as he rounded the wagon.

Was that disapproval in his voice? She had a sudden urge to run back to her room and bolt the door. At school she'd always known exactly what to do. Here, she felt like a fish on a grassy bank, wriggling and its mouth gaping for water.

When Jason drew closer, his chilly smile disappeared and some other expression stilled his face. His eyes were gray and deep, surrounded by small lines from hours of squinting in the sun. He had a small scar on his left cheekbone. Two seconds and the moment passed. He helped her into the buckboard, and they set off.

"We'll have to stop for Ma and Lucy," he told her as he guided the horses around the curve in the driveway and through the gate. Today was already warmer than yesterday. The sun made the top of her head feel warm beneath her hat. She raised the parasol and let it rest against her shoulder.

"Do they live far from here?" she asked.

"On the eastern corner of the ranch," he replied. "We have a cabin near a stand of trees with a stream running through it. Corky's cabin is within sight of ours."

He went on. "A few years back, Rudolph deeded each family the ten acres surrounding our homes." He gazed at her. "He was a good man, Sharon."

"I wouldn't be here if he wasn't, Jason," she said softly. "He was very kind to me, generous and considerate. I only wish I could have known him, too."

"It would have been good for Rudolph to have met you," he said. "He tried to help a couple of young people and ended up being disappointed." He smiled at her. "But he wouldn't have been disappointed in you."

three

Twenty minutes later, the Riordan cabin came into view. It was smaller than Uncle Rudolph's house, but it had a more steeply pitched roof. A stone fireplace almost covered one end of the building.

"When I became foreman two years ago, I moved into the bunkhouse," he told her. "Ma's arthritis flares up every now and then, so I still sleep here some nights to give Lucy a hand." He looped the reins over the whipstand and stepped to the ground.

The cabin door opened to reveal a slim girl wearing a blue gingham dress and a white cotton bonnet. She had dark hair and quick eyes. "Hello, Jason," she said, giving him a brief hug. "Mother is having a bad day. She said for us to go on without her."

Gazing intently through the cabin door, Jason asked, "Is she in bed?"

His sister nodded.

"I'll say hello to her before we go." He hurried inside, and Lucy moved toward the wagon.

Crossing a small field, Roddy and Mike McCormick ran toward the wagon. From their intent faces and long strides, they appeared to be racing.

Looking away from the boys, Sharon smiled at Jason's sister and said, "Good morning."

Lucy paused. "How do you do? I'm afraid Jason left without introducing us. I'm Lucy Riordan."

"It's good to meet you, Lucy. I'm so glad to meet someone my age."

She came closer. "I know. At least Ma and I can keep each other company. You've had to go it alone in the male world over there."

The McCormick boys scrambled in to the back of the buckboard, panting and arguing between breaths about who won. Lucy laughed at them. Sharon laughed, too.

"Have you met Roddy and Mike?" Lucy asked.

Sharon nodded. "Yes. Yesterday."

The next moment Jason dashed out and helped Lucy to the buckboard seat between him and Sharon.

Corky and his missus arrived at a more sedate pace and took the second seat. He introduced Sharon to Mrs. McCormick, a small woman with a shy demeanor. As the buckboard lurched forward, she turned and shushed the boys from their wrangling. Immediately, they went silent.

Lucy was a lively girl with a sparkle in her eye. "What do you do for fun?" she asked Sharon.

"Fun?" Sharon tried to find a quick answer but came up blank.

"What do you like to do? Grow things? Cook? Sew?" Lucy smiled. "I quilt, and I draw." She grimaced. "Not that I'm any kind of an artist." She plucked at Jason's coat sleeve. "My big brother buys me paper."

He grinned at her, a softness on his face and in his eyes.

"I like to paint with watercolors," Sharon announced with great relief. "I have a set of paints. You must come and see them."

"Watercolors!" Lucy gasped. "I've never actually seen a set. Could I come this afternoon?"

Jason sent her a warning look. "Lucy—"

"That would be wonderful," Sharon interrupted before he could squelch the idea. "I'd love for you to come."

Lucy's smile faded. "I may have to stay with Ma. She was

hurting something awful this morning. The pain seems to be worse when she's alone."

"I'll stay with her this afternoon," Jason said. "I'll read to her. She likes that."

"You're a dear!" Lucy leaned against him in a kind of sideways hug.

Jason turned to ask Corky a question about the ranch, and Lucy kept Sharon busy with questions about boarding school for the rest of the trip.

※

The church was a whitewashed stucco structure. Inside was a double column of wooden benches with low backs on them and a platform at the front that rose about a foot from the floor. The pulpit was a square, slanted board on top of a single post attached to the platform.

Sharon sat wedged between Lucy and a blond-haired young man. Lucy briefly introduced him as Timothy Ingles.

"Glad to know you, Miss Hastings," he said. About Sharon's age, he had wide-set blue eyes and a friendly, boyish mouth. "I believe I saw you the day you arrived."

"Do you work at the general store?" Sharon asked. When he nodded, she said, "Yes. I do remember you. You were standing outside the store when I first got here."

He blushed and suddenly seemed about twelve years old.

Looking toward the front, Lucy held her finger to her lips. The song leader had come to the pulpit to begin the service. Everyone in the pews had his or her own copy of the hymnbook. Sharon shared with Lucy.

The Reverend Nelson looked like he could have been a cowboy at one time; he was muscular and tall with a full, dark beard. He had a voice that came from deep within his massive chest and a powerful message that came from deep within his soul. Sharon lost track of time. She had received

Christ as a child of six. The boarding school was a Christian establishment, but it was Christian only in form and rules. The daily chapel sessions were dry and boring, and church was a time to sit next to her best friend, Candace, and study the clothes of everyone in attendance for later discussion.

This service was much different. There was life in the message and power in the Word like she hadn't felt for years. After the service, she shook the preacher's hand. "Thank you for that message," she said.

He smiled. "Welcome to Farmington, Miss Hastings," he said. "I trust you will find it a blessing."

"It already has been," she told him.

Lucy stayed beside Sharon, making introductions so fast that Sharon's mind reeled.

A man not much more than Sharon's height of five feet six paused near the girls. What he lacked in height, he surpassed in width.

"This is Jim Boswell," Lucy said. "He's the local blacksmith."

The stout man shook her hand and smiled with his pudgy, wet mouth. "I'm delighted to meet you, Miss Hastings." He ended the sentence with a short wheeze. "I blacksmith for the Lazy H from time to time." He had an anxious look on his face. He wheezed again and his thick neck convulsed as he swallowed. "I—I was wondering—if it would be agreeable to you if I were to come and call on you next Saturday."

Sharon blinked. She'd never had a man ask to call on her before. What should she say? Wanting to say no but not sure how, she said, "I would be honored, Mr. Boswell. Would three o'clock be a good time for you?"

His head bobbed. "Thank you, Miss Hastings." He backed away for two steps, then turned and headed for the wagons.

Lucy giggled. "I think you've made a conquest already," she said.

Sharon sent her an alarmed look.

Lucy went on, "Oh, there's my friend, Julia. You've got to meet her." She hurried away. Sharon followed, but at a sedate walk, according to Mrs. Minniver's Rule 10.

By the time they reached the buckboard, Sharon had a throbbing headache. The sun made her dress feel sticky. She found it hard to breathe.

They set off at a brisk pace. The breeze felt so refreshing. Lucy untied her bonnet and took it off to let the wind blow in her dark hair. Sharon wished she could do the same, but she couldn't force herself to ignore Rule 9.

After saying good-bye to the McCormick family and Jason, Lucy drove the buckboard to the ranch house. What a relief to step out of the sun.

After getting drinks for both of them from the pump in the kitchen, Sharon said, "If you don't mind, I'm going to get out of this hot dress. I'm about to suffocate."

Lucy laughed. "Of course. I don't know how you can take this heat, wearing silk."

Heading for her room, Sharon paused to say, "This will be the last time you see me in anything but cotton for a long time, I promise you."

A few minutes later, she rejoined Lucy at the dining room table. Max had left several bowls of food in the center of the table, covered by a large towel. On Sunday mornings, he cooked all of the food for that day so he could have a half day off. Today, he'd prepared a large pot containing potatoes, green beans, and pork. It didn't look like much, but it tasted great.

After the meal, Sharon brought her paints and sketchbooks to the table. Lucy sat speechless as Sharon showed them to her.

"You are an artist," Lucy breathed, staring wide-eyed at a painting of a puppy playing with an old shoe.

"That's a copy of a painting my teacher set up for us in the art room," Sharon said. "I copied the light and shadows from the other artist, so it's not really that good."

"That may be so, but it looks almost real. You should frame it and hang it up."

Sharon shrugged. "Maybe someday. Right now, I'm still trying to decide if I want to stay on here or sell the ranch to someone who can run it better than I can."

Lucy looked up, horrified. "Sell the ranch?" She reached out to clutch Sharon's hand. "You mustn't, Sharon. You mustn't."

Sharon became alarmed. "Why not, Lucy?"

"If you sell, Jason may lose his job. Who would support me and Ma? And what about Corky and his family? Where would they go?"

"Do you think that would happen?" Sharon asked, dismayed. "Why wouldn't they stay on and work for the new owner?"

"When the Widow Braddock sold her ranch, the new owner brought in his own crew. Everyone down to the cook had to find a new job. They all ended up going to Texas. My best friend, Sally, was the foreman's daughter."

"Lucy, I'm so sorry!" Sharon told her about Candace Matthews and how much she missed her best friend.

"I knew we were kindred spirits," Lucy declared when Sharon had finished. "I knew it right away."

Sharon laughed. "I've been here for two days now, and I haven't been to the barn. Would you mind walking out with me?" she asked. "I want to look at the horses."

"So do I," Lucy said. "When we were kids, Jason and I used to hang around the stables almost every day, but lately I haven't had any time."

They strolled outside and entered the wide barn. It was

dim and cool inside with the smell of cattle and straw pervading the massive structure. A long row of stalls ran its length. They were all empty.

Hearing faint mews, Sharon went for a closer look. In a corner of one stall, a black cat lay nursing four medium-size kittens.

"Aren't they cute!" she exclaimed.

"Be careful about touching them," Lucy warned. "Their mother isn't too friendly. She's a barn cat with long claws. I speak from experience." She moved to the half door in the back. "You can see the horses from here."

Sharon left the kittens and joined her.

Ten horses, mostly mustangs, browsed the grass or stood head to tail with a friend, swishing flies off each other.

Lucy named them off, ending with, "Maribell is the little black. She's going to foal any day."

"I can't wait to ride," Sharon told her. "It seems like forever since I've been in a real saddle in the open pasture."

"We should go riding sometime," Lucy said, smiling widely.

"Let me know when you are free and we'll go," Sharon promised.

They lingered for a few more minutes, then Lucy said, "We need to check the time. I can't be away too long with Ma so poorly today."

As they entered the house, the thirty-day clock on the mantel shelf chimed three times.

"I'd best get back to the house," Lucy said regretfully. "I put hot compresses on Ma's knees when she's hurting bad. She may need me."

"How about if I walk home with you? We can talk on the way." Sharon hurried to fetch her cotton sunbonnet and they set off.

As they meandered down the narrow dirt road, Sharon said, "When can you come back for another visit, Lucy?"

"How about if you take Sunday dinner with us next week?"

"Won't that be too much trouble for you?" Sharon asked. "You've got a lot on you, Lucy. I don't want to add to it."

"Oh, no," Lucy said. "I always get up early to cook. Jason usually stays for dinner after church, too." She swung her bonnet against her side. "Besides, Ma has a hankering to meet you. She was the one that made Rudolph give you an allowance, you know."

"She was?"

Lucy nodded, smiling as though she were telling a deep secret. "When Rudolph got word about the deaths in your family and your being orphaned and all, he was in a dither. He had no wife and no one to take care of a little girl. So, he talked to Ma about it. She told him what to do and how much money to send you, too." She laughed, delighted. "Later, Ma told us that she'd picked a number and then doubled it, to be sure you'd be taken care of proper. She couldn't stand to think that a poor little girl would be left with nothing and no one, all alone in a boarding school."

"This is the first I've ever heard of that," Sharon said. "I owe your mother more than I can say. Uncle Rudolph was very generous to me, and I'm so grateful. I wish I could have known him."

"He was a crusty old codger," Lucy said, "but underneath he was pure gold. He truly tried to help people be better than they were."

Sharon let a few paces pass in silence, then said, "Your brother seems kind of sad or troubled, Lucy. Is he always like that?"

She nodded. "He's been that way ever since Pa died." She shrugged. "Well, not all the time. He does laugh sometimes, but it's always with a little bit of sadness in it. You know what I mean? He worries about Ma. Since Rudolph's been gone, Jason's been full of worries. He's been sick with wondering what happened to Rudolph. And now he's got to run the ranch, take care of me and Ma, and wonder what to do if we have to leave the Lazy H. It's too much for a man who's barely twenty-five."

Sharon didn't reply. Watching the path ahead, she put one foot in front of the other. Would the Riordans and McCormicks have to leave? Would she?

four

A few minutes later, Sharon said good-bye to Lucy without going inside the Riordan's cabin. If Mrs. Riordan was in that much pain, Sharon didn't want to disturb her.

Still thinking about their conversation, she headed back down the trail. What an interesting girl Lucy was. They were going to be close friends. She knew it.

Jason caught up to Sharon before she reached the edge of the Riordan's yard. "Mind if I walk with you?" he asked, swinging his black broadcloth coat over his shoulder.

"Not at all." She kept her pace the same, not hurrying but moving along at a good clip.

They walked in silence for a while. Jason Riordan was evidently a man of few words. She may as well get used to it.

Finally, Sharon summoned up enough courage to say, "Jason, I want you to know something."

He turned toward her but didn't reply.

Something held her back. She couldn't say what she really wanted to tell him—that she didn't want to do anything that would force his family to leave the ranch. Finally, she went on, "I'm going to need your help, Jason. I want to learn as much as I can about every detail of this place. You're the one to teach me."

He stopped and turned back. She glanced at him, wondering what he was doing.

"The Colorado line is about fifteen miles straight north," he said, pointing. "See the mountains?"

Self-conscious, she turned to gaze at them, jagged and dark

in the distance. "I came through them on the train."

In a moment, they continued down the path, and he went on: "East and south are more of the same thing you see here—brush and grass and scattered trees. Five miles beyond our south fence line is the San Juan River."

He pointed west. "Over there's the water hole. Beyond that, the grass turns to scrub brush and the trees disappear. It's the edge of the desert, the home of the Navajo."

"Indians?"

He nodded. "Good people. All they're worried about is growing corn and weaving blankets. Totally different from their Texas cousins."

She breathed deeply of the clear air. "I really like it here," she said. "It's so peaceful."

Scanning the horizon, he murmured, "We all do. . .we all do."

When they reached the house, he dipped his head and tugged the brim of his hat. "Good afternoon, Sharon," he said. "We'll ride out after breakfast." He strode toward the bunkhouse without looking back.

Sharon slowly untied her bonnet strings as she trudged inside. Did he naturally dislike her? No matter what she said or what he replied, she felt like she was on trial. She wished she could have Max take her to see the ranch. He was much nicer than Jason Riordan.

೩

The sky was a faded blue gray when Jason and Sharon mounted up the next morning. Jason had brought her a roan mare named Springtime. The horse was sweet and gentle, the perfect mount for a lady.

Dressed in a wide split skirt that fell in deep folds around her in the saddle, Sharon was thrilled to be on horseback. She gripped the reins and squeezed with her knees. As her horse cantered neck and neck with Jason's gelding, Sharon couldn't stop an exhilarated laugh.

"We'll ride the fence line to start out," he said when they pulled up. "Then I'll take you to the water hole. That's all we'll have time for before lunch."

"Next time, bring me a horse with more spirit," she told him. "I grew up helping my father train horses, and I like them lively." She patted the mare's neck. "Which way?"

He nodded east. "That's the closest boundary to the house. We'll start there."

She didn't wait for him to say more. She urged the mare to a faster pace than before and didn't slow down until silvery barbed wire glinted ahead of her.

Laughing from sheer joy, she tried to catch her breath. Jason was grinning like an impudent schoolboy, but he didn't say anything. He dealt out words like they were silver dollars.

Walking the horses along the fence for a few minutes to let them cool off, Jason and Sharon rode apart. Sharon let her eyes feast on the vastness of the land surrounding her. There wasn't a man made structure as far as she could see. The wind rustled through a small grove of desert willows. It lifted the brim of her bonnet and cooled her face.

This section of the land was grassy and rolling with small groves of trees here and there. Longhorns grazed in the distance.

"There's a stream up ahead that goes behind Ma's cabin," Jason said. "It's a fork off the big creek that comes down from the north. The main creek continues southwest and just about splits the ranch in half."

The stream was narrow, but its banks were four feet high in some places. Now and then a stretch of bank had been dug down, so cattle could drink from it.

For half an hour they followed the stream northwest until

it joined a wider body of water flowing south.

"Our fence line is about three hundred yards north of this fork," Jason told her. "If we followed the fence on around to the west, we'd pass through the edge of the desert. That side meets the Navajo Reservation. Fall is the best time to go over there. It's much too hot and dry this time of year."

"I'm trying to comprehend how big this place is," she said, straining to see far into the distance. "How can three men handle all of this land?"

"We hire extra hands for roundup and the cattle drive, the busiest time of the year," he said. "Otherwise, we're doing maintenance, and three men can handle it. Corky's boys take care of the barn, mucking out the stalls and all."

She studied him. "I've heard of a roundup, but I've never understood how it works."

He spent the next ten minutes explaining the process of gathering the herd, branding the calves, and moving the yearlings to the railroad where they could be sold. "We usually manage to make enough from the cattle drive to finance the rest of the year."

"And if we don't?" Sharon asked.

"Rudolph has a long-standing account at the Farmington National Bank. If we run short, he goes in and adds a little to the mortgage to tide us over. If we have extra, he goes in and pays some of it off. Every once in a while, he'll sell some of the breeding stock and buy new blood to keep the herd strong. We usually make a little extra doing that, too."

"How much is the mortgage?"

He shook his head. "That's something you'll have to find out at the bank. I have no idea."

She said, "He paid for my schooling and sent me a generous allowance even when he was short here? Why would he do that for a child he'd never met?"

Jason's eyes narrowed. "You never met him?"

"He moved to New Mexico before I was born. My parents exchanged letters with him, but I never saw him myself."

"Were he and your father close?"

She nodded. "They were two years apart. Uncle Rudolph was older, and he always took care of my father. A few times he sent us money to help us out of a tough spot. Pa never said much about money, but once I heard him talking to Mama about it after I was in bed.

"Pa practically worshiped Uncle Rudolph. From what Mama said, he was pretty lost when Rudolph decided to go west."

"Why didn't your father come here to join his brother instead of heading to Oregon?"

She slowly shook her head. "I'm not sure, Jason. My folks didn't tell me much about what they had in mind. I was only thirteen at the time."

They topped a rise and an oval-shaped pond came into view. The ground around it was hard packed; there was little grass anywhere around.

"This is the famous Lazy H water hole," he said with a touch of pride in his voice. "It's a little over four feet deep at the center and about fifty feet across. One of the first things Rudolph did when he came to these parts was to dig it out, so it would hold more water and last through the dry months."

"You grew up here, didn't you?"

He nodded. "Do you want to walk a little?"

She swung down with no help from him. Looping the ends of the reins over their pommels, they let the horses drink.

As though the conversation had never paused, Jason said, "My parents were married after my pa had worked here about two years. I grew up running all over this range, like Corky's boys do now. Rudolph was like a second father to me."

"Like an uncle?" she asked.

He glanced at her. "I reckon that's right."

"That's ironic. He was my uncle in blood but your uncle in fact."

"He was a godly man, Sharon. He loved God, and he tried to help people. I think that's why his life was so blessed."

"You're a believer?" she asked.

"I accepted the Lord when I was fifteen." His lips twisted into a wry grin. "I was a bounder before that. It was Rudolph who took me aside and told me I was headed for a bad end." He took off his hat and tapped it against the side of his leg. "He was right."

"I was saved when I was six," Sharon said, "but since my parents died, I haven't thought about it much. The boarding school was a Christian institution run by two sisters: Miss Oliver and Mrs. Minniver. But they didn't emphasize religion much. We had morning prayers and went to church, but that was all. I used to pray before I went to sleep that God would bless Uncle Rudolph and help the days fly past until I could come and live with him here."

"God did bless him," Jason said. "You weren't the only one he helped, either. He set up Timothy Ingles's father, Zach, in the Farmington General Store and helped him run it until Zach got his feet under him." He kicked at a clump of scrub grass. "Ingles had been in trouble with the law sometime back, but Rudolph saw something in the man."

"I wish I could have known my uncle," Sharon murmured. "If not for him, I'd have gone to an orphanage. Now I can't even thank him."

"If he saw how you'd turned out, that would be thanks enough," Jason said. His face still had that guarded expression, but his eyes were alive. "Don't worry about the ranch. I'll carry the load for you, Sharon. I give you my word on that."

She put out her hand to shake his. "Thank you, Jason. I'm going to depend on that."

He seemed to forget that he still held her gloved hand as he stared at the darkening sky. "There's gonna be a gully washer," he said. "They come up fast in these parts. We'd best head for home." He whistled. Both horses lifted their heads and came toward him.

They rushed for their saddles. He held his hands together to give Sharon a leg up, then mounted his own horse.

"Who's your horse trainer?" Sharon called to him. "He knows his business."

"Max."

"Max?"

He chuckled. "When he's not slinging hash, he's in the corral. Didn't he tell you that?" He laughed at her shocked reaction. At that moment, a cold wind swept across the range. The soft, deep sigh of thunder spurred them to a gallop.

Ten minutes later, the first fat drops splattered on the mare's neck. With a whoop, Jason veered onto a wide trail. Sharon kept the mare at full gallop to keep pace with his gelding.

When the torrent broke loose, Jason reined in a little to let her come up beside him. "Do you want to find shelter?" he hollered.

"How far are we from home?" She blinked to see him through the hazy cloud of falling water. Her chin was dripping.

"It's another twenty minutes if we keep moving."

"Let's keep on going!" she called. "Why be miserable longer than we have to be?"

He leaned over the horse's neck and let out another whoop. The gelding raced down the trail. The mare did her best to keep up, but she was no match for Jason's horse.

Sharon tucked her chin down, so the rain would fall away

from her face. Cold, damp fingers trickled down her spine. Her shoulders hunched against the chill. She tried not to shiver. Her bonnet brim hung limply before her eyes.

Trusting her mount to find the way home, she simply held on and prayed for the ride to be over.

They heard the call for lunch as they rode into the yard. Jason grabbed her horse's reins and guided the mare to the edge of the porch so Sharon could dismount directly to its high floor.

Max stood near the triangle at the corner of the porch. He hurried toward her. "I'll fetch you some towels!" he called and trotted inside. He met her at the door with five of them.

Peeling off her bonnet, she let it drop to the porch floor and wrapped her head in one of the towels. Blotting her face, she took the other towels and hustled into her room to peel off her sodden clothes.

Was there anything more miserable? How could one be soaking wet and yet feel so filthy?

Shivering, she took a few minutes to sponge off in the basin. Then she loosened her blond hair and combed it out. If she wanted to join the men for lunch, she'd have to go out there with a wet head. There was nothing she could do about it besides have Max bring her a plate in her room. The last thing she wanted was to act like a prima donna before the men.

She stared at herself in the mirror. Did it really matter that much? "Mrs. Minniver is in Springfield, you goose. You're home." Her chin quivered as she spoke. "Stop acting like she's still your headmistress." With shaking hands, she pulled her hair to the front and wove a loose braid that came over her shoulder. She got into a thick dress of blue twill and found some wool socks. It was June, and she'd probably regret the warm clothes ten minutes after putting them on, but she was freezing now, and that's all that mattered.

When Sharon reached the table, the men were already eating.

"Don't get up," she told them, taking her seat. "Max, could I have some hot coffee?"

"You look chilled to the bone, child," he said, handing her a steaming cup. "It's not that cold out, is it? It's pretty warm inside today."

Sipping, she nodded. "I'll be okay once I warm up. We were riding fast and getting wet at the same time. That's what got me chilled." She breathed in the warmth spiraling up from her mug. Sipping again, she felt the hot liquid soothing her inside.

Max filled her plate with stew and placed a biscuit on the rim.

Wilson finished the last of his stew with a large mouthful and stood. "Jason'll need a hand with those ho'ses," he said. Striding to a row of pegs beside the door, he lifted his tattered gray Stetson and ducked out into the weather.

"Where did you ride?" Max asked, taking his seat.

"We went around the fence line behind the cabins and then over to the water hole. When it started pouring, we headed home." She put down her spoon. "I can't get over how big the ranch is. It's enormous."

Corky chuckled. "Pardon my saying so, but you only saw half of it, maybe less."

Sharon looked up to see the third McCormick boy sitting next to his father with his brothers lined up beside him. He was smaller and darker than his brothers. "Hello," she said to the boy. "We haven't met yet, have we?"

He shook his head.

Corky gave him an elbow in the ribs.

"No, miss," the boy said, his cheeks pink.

"This is Ian," Corky said. "He's thirteen."

The boy's freckled face turned brilliant red, and he bent his head down. Roddy snickered.

Corky chuckled.

The door opened, and Jason strode inside wearing a dripping yellow slicker. He hung it on a peg and topped it with his hat. His shirt looked fresh, but his jeans and boots were still wet. He ran his hands along the sides of his head, smoothing his wet hair away from his face.

"Thanks, Max," he said, dropping to a seat as the little man handed him a cup of coffee. "That rain'll chill you clean through." He glanced at Sharon. "Are you all right?"

Sipping coffee, she nodded. "Now I am."

He drank some black coffee, then dug into the stew.

"The boys and I will clean the tack room this afternoon," Corky said.

Chewing a biscuit, Jason nodded, then swallowed. "Knock off whenever there's a break in the rain," he said. "The sky's so dark it may rain all night. If you wake up to rain in the morning, take the day off."

Jason finished his meal without saying anything more to her. After the others had left the table, they still sat in silence.

"Thank you for taking me out today," she said finally.

"That's what I'm here for," he said, glancing in her general direction. "We'll ride south when there's a good day for it. Not as much to see that way, though." He drained his cup and stood. "Max, I think the little mustang mare is going to foal any time."

Max left the dishpan and buried his wet hands in his apron. He turned away for a second to cough. Clearing his throat, he nodded. "I'll come out and take a look at her when I get a chance," he said.

Jason nodded. He gave Sharon a casual two-fingered salute as he headed for the door.

Sharon dragged off to her room. Her riding clothes lay in a puddle on the floor. Throwing her wash water out the window, she gathered the wet clothes into a ball and plopped them into the basin. There would be time to deal with those later. At this moment, she had to get under the quilt and rest her eyes. She pulled off the twill dress and slid into her cotton nightgown.

The sheets welcomed her. The down pillow cradled her head. Yet, strangely, the rest she craved slipped out of her reach. Why had Jason ignored her at lunch? They'd had such a good talk at the water hole.

Jason Riordan was a fine man. She was blessed to have him as foreman. She could see that clearly. But he was so distant, so guarded most of the time. Why didn't he like her?

ã

Outside the house, a big cowboy wearing a yellow slicker stood on the edge of the porch and gazed across the yard. He ought to get to the bunkhouse and change into dry clothes. His mother would have a conniption if she knew he was standing here in wet jeans and soaked boots.

He stood there, unmoving, staring at the silvery curtain surrounding the house. It sometimes moved with the breeze and doused him with spray. He didn't feel the wind or the damp. All he could see were cheeks like fine china, green eyes with a spark like flint on stone, and those soft, quivering lips against the coffee cup. If only she hadn't taken down her blond hair. If she hadn't done that, he would have been all right.

Drawing in a long breath, he adjusted his hat and stepped into the rain.

five

Late Friday evening, everyone was on the front porch, enjoying the first cooling breezes of the sweltering day. Sharon and Max sat on the bench, Jason on a chair brought from the kitchen, and Wilson on the step.

"Did you see this?" Wilson asked no one in particular. "The bottom step is loose." He wiggled it with his foot. "Looks like it's fixing to split down the middle." He bent over to tug on it. "We can't have that. I'll have to fix it next chanc't I get."

Jason said, "The parson called on Ma and Lucy this afternoon. They're having a prayer meeting at the church on Saturday night." He looked around. "Anyone else want to go?"

Sharon felt a squeezing in her chest, that awful feeling that she was forgetting something. She knew she had something to do on Saturday. What was it?

"Not me," Wilson drawled. "The Almighty would be shocked to see me after all these years."

"I don't have anything better to do," Max said. "I'll come along."

Jason turned to Sharon.

"What time would we leave?" she asked.

"Five o'clock, I reckon."

Sharon felt a jolt. Jim Boswell was coming to call at three o'clock. She stifled a relieved laugh. That meant he'd only stay for two hours. She could deal with him for that long, surely.

"Is Lucy going to the prayer meeting?" she asked.

"Lucy and Ma, too, as long as she's up to it."

"Good." She turned to Max. "I think I'll bake some molasses

cookies in the morning. Jim Boswell is coming out tomorrow afternoon."

Wilson came alert. "Is he now? Maribell has a shoe that needs to be checked."

Jason let out a hoot. "Sorry, Wilson. Blacksmithing is gonna be the last thing on his mind."

Wilson looked confused.

Sharon's face was on fire. She stood, said good night, and made a hasty escape. The laughter of the three men followed her into the house.

❧

And their smiling didn't stop there. It lasted through Saturday's breakfast and got worse at lunch.

Clearing the table, Sharon asked Max, "Why is Jim Boswell's visit such a joke?"

Max chuckled. "You really don't know, do you?" When she shook her head, he went on, "You're way above his league, Sharon. Why on earth did you agree to see him?"

Sharon stiffened. "He came up to me after church last Sunday. He was so nervous that I felt sorry for him. I couldn't think of a way to say no without seeming rude." She let out a moan. "How did I get myself into this? We can't go riding because we're going to be leaving for church at five. What are we going to do while he's here?"

Max's thick teeth gleamed. "Feed him cookies. He'll stay as happy as a goose in a corncrib."

As soon as Max had cleared away the lunch dishes, Sharon mixed a triple batch of molasses cookies. Whatever Jim left, the men would clear up in short order.

When Jim arrived, she was wearing a dress of pink gingham and a fresh white apron. Pressed and polished in a white shirt, he had on a black string tie, pressed pants, and gleaming boots. His face glowed from a recent scrubbing.

"Good afternoon, Miss Sharon," he said when she answered the door.

"Hello, Jim. Won't you come in?"

He stood uncertainly just inside the door, his felt hat in his thickly calloused hands.

Sharon smiled in his direction. "May I take your hat?" she asked, then hung it on a peg. "The house is too warm this time of day. I set some chairs outside the back door in the shade." She led the way through the kitchen and down the back step.

The wide limbs of a cottonwood tree made a perfect shady spot for their visit, especially because it was out of range of the prying eyes of the smirking ranch hands.

At least Jim Boswell knew how to hold polite conversation. They talked of local news, that evening's prayer meeting, and Jim's work while he munched cookies and drank buttermilk.

"Have you ever heard of the Cattleman's Treasure?" he asked her.

"I heard someone mention it."

He reached for another cookie. "It's a legend, or a myth, or something in these parts. No one knows what it is, but it's supposed to be on this ranch somewhere."

"As far as I know, Uncle Rudolph never told anyone what it was. We'll probably never know."

Finally, Max came to the back door. "Jason's bringing up the buckboard," he said. He coughed and tapped his chest. "He'll be here in a few minutes."

Sharon tried to hide her relief. "Thank you, Max. We'll be right there."

She walked with Jim through the house to the front porch. The afternoon sun shone into the porch and made her blink. Off to the left, a fly buzzed. Corky's boys played catch under the shade of the giant cottonwood in the front yard.

"Thank you for a pleasant afternoon," Jim said, beaming at her. "I hope I can call again sometime."

"Thank you for coming," Sharon replied, careful not to commit herself this time. She handed him his hat, and he headed down the stairs.

Suddenly, his arms flew out, and his hat went flying. He let out a loud cry and tumbled forward. His shiny boots came up and his shiny face hit the ground. Rolling over twice, he came to a stop in the driveway.

The boys roared with laughter. Ian threw himself on the ground while Roddy and Mike reared their heads and howled.

Her heart pounding, Sharon started down the steps toward Jim until Max cried, "Look out!" and she drew up short.

The bottom step wasn't broken or loose anymore. It was gone.

At that moment, Wilson came out of the barn at a trot with a weathered piece of wood in his hands. He was in such a hurry that he stepped on a kitten's tail. With a snarl, the cat streaked into the safety of the barn.

Sharon raised her skirts a little and stepped gingerly to the ground.

"Jim!" she cried when she finally reached him. "Are you all right?"

Muttering, he slowly got to his feet. His face was the color of an old brick. His eyebrows drew down until his eyes almost disappeared. "Who was the stupid. . ." He let off a string of words that made Sharon gasp.

Wilson reached them as Jim ran out of breath. The cowhand held up the plank in his hands. "I took the step to the barn to add some support," he said, turning it over. On the bottom was a neat strip of new wood across the middle. "I'm sorry, hombre," he said to Jim. He gave the blacksmith a hand up. "No harm done?" He turned toward the still-hooting boys and gave them a sign to cut it out.

Sharon turned to stare at Max. "You just came up those steps, didn't you?"

He held his hands up, palms out. "I stopped to take care of something in the kitchen and plumb forgot to tell him." He looked at Jim. "My apologies, Boswell," he said.

Sharon turned to look Wilson in the eye. The cowhand was all sober-faced concern.

Ignoring them all, Jim turned his attention toward beating his dusty clothes. Finally, he picked up his hat, gave Sharon a nod, and headed for his horse where it was ground-hitched under the tree.

At that moment, Jason and Corky pulled up in the buckboard and Max climbed aboard. Wilson helped Sharon up and stood back as the McCormick boys scrambled over the tailgate. No one spoke a word until Boswell's horse disappeared in a cloud of dust.

Roddy started with a little giggle, followed by Ian's chuckle. The next moment, every male in the wagon was guffawing and slapping each other.

"Did you men cook that up to embarrass me?" she demanded. "What were you thinking of? Jim could have been hurt."

Max took a breath to say, "Only his pride, Sharon. And he's got plenty of that to spare." He slapped his knee and laughed again, ending with a coughing spell.

Sharon tried to squelch her smile, but her lips wouldn't cooperate. Several times after the prayer meeting had ended that evening, she had to chuckle to herself. Those men seemed tough and hard, but they were nothing but big boys.

Shortly after dark, a cool wind came up, followed by a thunderstorm that shook the house. Alone in the house, Sharon stood by the window and watched lightning streak across the black sky, thrilled at the glory of it. She stayed there until it stopped, then went to bed and fell into a dreamless sleep.

✍

The next morning, Sharon came out of her room to find Jason in the kitchen, looking in the cabinets. He'd already built a fire in the cookstove.

He paused when he saw her. "Max's sick," he said. "He's burning up with fever and shaking with chills by spells." He lifted a yellow crockery bowl of day-old biscuits and set it on the counter. "He was up most of the night with Maribell in foal and got soaked to the hide, going back and forth to the barn." Jason's eyes had dark rings around them like he hadn't slept much either.

"It's still raining," he went on. "Lucy usually helps out at times like this, but she can't get here in the rain." He shrugged. "It's just as well. Ma's arthritis is awful bad in this weather. It'll only be you, me, and Wilson to meals. Corky's staying at home today."

Sharon rolled up her sleeves. "I'm not much of a cook," she said, stepping forward, "but I think I can get us through breakfast if we have any eggs."

He turned full circle and spotted a basket of eggs in the corner. "Max keeps ten chickens in a coop out back."

"Max is a marvel," Sharon said, reaching for the basket. "Could you fetch me some milk?"

"The springhouse," he said. He disappeared out the back door and was soon back with a jar of milk. He lifted the lid and sniffed. "It smells a little sour."

"I can still use it."

He stood in the center of the room, arms at his sides, with an uncertain look on his face.

"You don't have to watch over me," she told him, whipping

milk into the eggs with a fork. "I can manage."

He looked relieved. "I've got chores in the barn," he said and headed for the door.

Sharon dumped out the old coffee grounds and rinsed the pot. She wasn't sure how much coffee to use, so she guessed. She found some brown paper, dampened it, and wrapped up the hardened biscuits left from yesterday's lunch.

By the time the hands arrived twenty minutes later, the omelets were ready, and the biscuits were soft and warm. The coffee, however, was lukewarm and weak as dishwater. Only Jason drank it.

As the men were leaving, Sharon said, "Jason, is there anything I can do for Max? Maybe we ought to bring him into the house where I can look after him."

"He's too sick to be moved in this rain," Jason replied, standing. "I wish the doc was handy. He's mighty bad."

"I'll go and take a look at him. At least I can make him more comfortable." She pushed back from the table. "Will you take me to him?"

"Of course. Let me go out and make sure he's awake and decent," he said. "I'll come and fetch you when he's ready for you to come in." He shrugged into his slicker and pulled the hood over his Stetson. The next moment he closed the door behind him.

Sharon washed the dishes while she waited. She dug around in the kitchen cabinet next to the back door and found some tonic, powdered mustard, and a small tin of black tea. That was all there was of any medicinal value whatsoever.

Whispering a prayer for guidance, she fetched her wool cape from her room and laid it across the back of the couch where it would be handy when Jason returned.

What would they eat for lunch and supper? How she wished the rain would stop so Lucy could come. Maybe she could ask Max for advice if he wasn't too sick to talk to her.

Spooning tea into a pint jug, she added hot water from the reservoir in the cookstove. At least she could take him some tea. Sick people needed plenty to drink.

She found a sack of rice beneath the counter. If she set on some beef to stew and made a gravy for it, they could eat beef and rice. She could manage that. They might be eating beef and rice for the next two or three days if it kept on raining. She didn't even know how to make johnnycake or biscuits. Bread was out of the question. Why hadn't she stuck closer to Mama in the kitchen instead of running out to the stable to help Pa with the horses?

Jason came in as she was measuring rice into a bowl. Two cups should be enough.

"Can you fetch me some beef?" she asked him. "Where does Max keep it?"

"There's a smokehouse out back," he told her. "I'll get you some." Lifting a metal basin from the counter, he stepped through the back door and returned in five minutes with a shapeless hunk of meat.

Setting it on the counter, he said, "Max says he doesn't want you to worry over him. He said he'll be all right in a couple of days."

"What about you?" she asked. "Do you think he'll be all right in a couple of days?"

He shook his head doubtfully. "I'm no doctor, but he looks bad to me."

"If he's that sick, he won't be able to make too much of a fuss about my coming out to see him then," she said. "If you'll lead the way, I'll come after you." She added two spoonfuls of sugar to the jug and strained the results into another small jar. Lifting a tin cup from a shelf, she turned it upside down over the top of the jar and wrapped the whole thing in a dish towel.

"Is that for him?" Jason asked. When she nodded, he picked it up.

Wrapping herself in the cape, she huddled down and ducked her head to hide under its hood. She followed Jason by watching his boots splashing across the yard.

Finally, he opened a door and let her pass him into the bunkhouse.

She stood dripping just inside the door. A few moments passed before her eyes could adjust to the dim light inside.

"I'll take your cape," Jason said, setting the jar on a ledge. He waited for her to hand the cape to him. "Max's cot is the last one on the left." He hung their wraps on pegs.

The room had cots along both walls, enough for a dozen hands in all. Two lanterns hung from square-headed nails in posts along the walls. The windows were high and small. The room felt drafty and damp. It smelled of coal oil and stale clothes.

Sharon moved down the center aisle and stopped beside Max's bed. Stooping down, she felt his dry, hot forehead. His eyes fluttered open. "Sharon, you shouldn't trouble yourself about me," he rasped. "I'll get over this in a day or so." He coughed weakly.

She knelt beside him. "It's no trouble, Max. I hate to admit it, but I came out to help myself as much as to check on you. I'm not much of a cook, you know." She looked up to meet Jason's worried gaze. "I came to ask a favor."

Max peered at her and tried to moisten his dry lips.

"Would you mind if Jason and Wilson brought you into the house? You could stay in one of the spare rooms. Then I can ask your advice about the meals. I'm afraid the men will starve to death if I don't get some help. Cooking has never been my strong point."

He drew in a labored breath. "I guess that would be all

right. I feel terrible about leaving you to do it all."

"I don't mind doing the work," she said. "That's not it at all. I'd feel better if you were nearby."

She tucked the blanket around him. "It's raining too hard for you to come in now. I brought you some tea. Try to drink it for me, will you? Then you can rest until the weather eases off. That'll give me a chance to get your bed ready."

Jason handed her the jar, then helped Max sit up enough to sip from the cup. Max gulped down half of it, then sank back. His eyes drifted closed.

"Could you stay with him and see if he can drink the rest of that cupful?" she asked. "I can get back to the house on my own."

Jason stood and followed her to the door. "When Wilson comes back from the barn, we can bring him in right on that cot," he whispered. "When it quits raining, we'll cover him up and haul him out."

She nodded as she fastened the clasp on her cape. "I only hope we can get him through this," she said. "Is there a doctor in Farmington?"

Jason nodded. "After we get Max inside, I'll send Wilson to fetch him."

Sharon hurried through the rain, dodging puddles and wincing at the sogginess of her shoes.

An hour later, the sun took a peek at them. The men arrived on the porch a few minutes later, Jason at the front and Wilson at the back of the cot. A tarpaulin covered Max from head to toe.

Sharon flung open the door to the front bedroom, and they marched inside. Within five minutes, the little man was in his new bed with a quilt tucked under his chin.

Following Jason out, she pulled the bedroom door closed. Now that she had Max in the house, she wasn't sure what to do with him. She had no medicine and knew precious little about nursing the sick.

"Wilson's going to fetch the doc," Jason told her. "If he's quick, they could be back in two or three hours."

"We'll pray they are," she said.

"Is there anything I can do to help you?" he asked as Wilson hurried away.

"If you have time on your hands, I could use some company in the kitchen," she admitted. "I've been hoping the rain would stop so Lucy could come. We'd have a good time working together."

"She'd like it," Jason said, smiling. "I'll fetch her as soon as it eases off again."

"Let me check on Max first," she said and eased his door open. He was sleeping soundly, a little gurgling rasp at the end of each breath.

Leaving the door ajar, so she could hear him if he called, Sharon joined Jason in the kitchen and picked up the basin of meat. "I guess I should cut this up into chunks and stew it. We can eat it over rice."

He pulled a knife from a sheath in his boot. "I can help you there," he said.

She stared doubtfully at the gleaming blade. "Where was that used last?" she asked.

He chuckled and ambled to the pitcher pump to wash it. "I guess all you womenfolk think alike. That's exactly what my ma would have said."

Sharon found a knife, and they sat at Max's worktable on the left side of the cooking fireplace. The tabletop was four inches of solid oak, worn and scarred from years of such abuse as they were working on it now.

In case Max was awake, she whispered, "I hope you don't think badly of me for telling Max that I needed his help. I do need advice, but I was really trying to get him to agree to come in without an argument."

Jason nodded. "You handled him like a lynx after a jackrabbit," he replied, his tone matching hers.

She looked up at him. "I'll take that as a compliment."

Still cutting, he grinned. "As intended."

As they worked, she asked a question that had been long on her mind. "Jason, what's the Cattleman's Treasure Uncle Rudolph talked about?"

He chuckled. "It may have been nothing but the good earth on the ranch. Rudolph liked to tease and that was one way he did it. You should have seen the men gathered around the potbelly stove at the general store when he'd start talking about his treasure. He wanted to get a rise out of them, and the Cattleman's Treasure did just that."

"I wish I knew what it was," she said, slicing a large onion.

"Don't we all?" They worked in silence for a few minutes, then Jason let out a soft chuckle.

Sharon glanced at him, surprised.

Softly, as though talking to himself, Jason said, "I sure wish I'd been close enough to get a look at Jim Boswell's face when he realized he'd stepped off into thin air."

Sharon's lips tightened. "You can be glad you didn't hear what Jim said when he hit the ground," she retorted. "I haven't heard that kind of language since I went with Pa to the beef auction in St. Louis when I was ten years old."

His expression brightened. "You don't say." Suddenly, he snapped his fingers into the air.

The move was so sudden that Sharon jumped. She glanced at him from the corner of her eye. Why was he so pleased?

six

In thirty minutes the beef was simmering on the stove, and the rice pot, too.

Sharon went to check on Max and found him awake. "Are you in pain, Max?" she asked, feeling his burning forehead.

"My chest hurts when I breathe."

"Wilson went to fetch the doctor. He should be back in an hour or so."

The sick man's eyes closed. "Too much trouble," he wheezed.

She turned to Jason standing in the bedroom doorway and said, "I feel so helpless. I'm afraid he has pneumonia. What would your mother do if she were here?"

"Her cure for everything is a good dose of castor oil and a hot toddy for a chaser." He stepped back. "Let's wait for the doc. He should be here soon."

He arrived twenty minutes later.

A short, wiry man with a long, bony nose, Dr. Lanchester was too old to be young and too young to be considered an old man. The deep creases on his thin face bore witness that he'd seen his share of life.

The moment he stepped inside, Jason ushered him into the sickroom. The doctor shooed everyone out and closed the door. Wilson peeled off his slicker and stood uncertainly at the door, his boots making twin pools on the plank flooring.

"The cookstove is hot," Sharon said. "Why don't you stand over it and get warm?" She hurried to bring him a towel.

"Much obliged, miss," he said.

"Who?" she asked with a small smile.

He grinned and his face went lopsided. "Sharon," he said, burying his grizzled face in the towel.

Sharon pulled a chair for Wilson close to the stove, then returned to the living room to sit on the sofa. "Do you think we should start a fire?" she asked. "It's not really cold, just a chilly dampness. I'm afraid we'll get too warm, but I'm miserable in this chill."

"How about if I start a little bitty one?" Jason asked. "One small log and a few branches. We can always kick it apart if it gets too warm, or open the front door for a spell."

She nodded. "It would chase out the dampness."

He seemed relieved to have something to do.

While Jason was still laying the wood, the doctor came out. His face was drawn.

"How is he, Doctor?" Sharon asked.

Lanchester shook his head. "It's touch and go," he replied. "He'll need someone with him around the clock." He pulled a pad of paper from his pocket and wrote on it. "Here's how to make a mustard plaster." He scribbled for a few seconds. "Keep changing it out every hour. Make him drink plenty—water, tea, anything he'll swallow. That's very important. He's dried out pretty bad."

Sharon took the paper from his hand. "Will you come back tomorrow?"

Shoving the pad of paper into his inner coat pocket, he nodded. "I've got office appointments in the morning, but I'll try to get out in the afternoon. If he should go out of his head with delirium, come and get me right away, day or night."

Jason shook his hand. "Thank you, Doc."

"You're welcome, Jason. How is your mother doing? I haven't seen her for a while."

"She's been having a lot of bad days lately, I'm afraid."

"When I come out tomorrow, I'll stop by the cabin and take a look at her."

"Thank you, Doctor," Sharon said.

"You're welcome, young lady," he said and hurried out.

When the door closed, Sharon gasped in alarm. "What about paying him? Am I supposed to pay him?"

Jason said, "Rudolph used to take him a quarter of beef every spring and that covered his services for the year. We won't owe him anything until next spring, the way I figure it."

She read the slip of paper. "I found some mustard in the kitchen that we can use. I hope it's enough."

He gazed at her. "Are you going to be able to handle all of this? Cooking and nursing besides?"

"I can manage for a day or two. What will your mother do if Lucy comes here? Can Lucy leave her?"

"Corky's wife will take care of Ma. When Lucy has to go somewhere, Corky's wife sends one of the boys to stay with Ma and sends over meals. They're good neighbors." He peered out the misty window. "Rain or no, I'm going to fetch Lucy tomorrow."

But later that day the rain stopped, and Lucy arrived at the ranch house before nightfall. Sharon wanted to cry from relief when her new friend came through the door.

Jason took his sister's coat and hung it up. "I've got to help Wilson with the chores," he told them. "I'll come in afterward." And he left.

"How is Max?" Lucy asked.

"He's in there." Sharon nodded toward the front room. "I've got to change his plaster in ten minutes."

"Show me what you're doing and I'll take over. You look all in."

Sharon tried out a weary smile. "If I could sleep for two hours, I'd be able to sit up with him tonight." She found the doctor's slip of paper. She told Lucy what he had said and showed her the mustard paste warming on the stove.

They changed the next plaster together, then Lucy sent Sharon to bed. Exhausted, Sharon changed into a gown and was asleep seconds after the quilt covered her.

A dim stream of light across her bed woke Sharon up. She rubbed her eyes and wondered if it were dusk or dawn. She splashed water on her face and pulled on a fresh housedress. The smell of biscuits and bacon told her she'd slept longer than she'd intended.

The sick vigil lasted for two more days. Finally, the fever broke, and Max started coughing in earnest. As painful as it was for him, they were all relieved to see him throwing off the infection. The following day, Dr. Lanchester declared him out of the woods.

Lucy stayed one more day after that.

While she was there, the girls had spent every spare moment in the kitchen with Lucy teaching Sharon how to cook. Within a few days, Sharon was well schooled in biscuit making, bread making, and the art of cooking beans. She could throw together a fine johnnycake, too. Sharon worked at cooking like she did everything else—with intense concentration and determination. She never wanted to feel so helpless in her own house again.

While Lucy was sleeping, Sharon dished up beans, beef, and biscuits for Max and poured him some hot tea.

He made a face when he picked up the blue enamel cup. "Don't you have any coffee?" he asked. "This is women's brew."

Sharon grinned at him. "You should be thankful. The last thing you want to drink is my coffee. I'm hoping you can help me make cowboy coffee when you get better. Lucy said she had no idea how you do it."

He savored a bite of a golden biscuit. "You'll be putting me out to pasture," he said after a moment. "These are better than mine."

"Not by a country mile," Sharon told him. She sat near him in the rocking chair. "You've still got a lot to teach me, Max. And I want to learn it all."

He chuckled and ended up coughing. Sipping tea, he drew in a breath and said, "When you first got here, you were so brittle I was afraid you'd break, but underneath all that boarding school polish was a real genuine lady. I only wish your uncle Rudolph could have been here to know you."

She felt a sweet warmth inside that blossomed into a wide smile. That was the kindest thing anyone had said to her since she'd arrived.

At that moment, she looked up to see Jason coming through the cabin doorway. He wasn't smiling at all.

seven

Jason had never liked or trusted Edward Kellerman. When he saw the lawyer riding into the ranch yard on that June afternoon, Jason wasn't happy. When old Stewart Pitt passed away two years before, Kellerman had appeared in town within a month to take over Pitt's practice. Always fawning over the women and flattering the men, he was altogether too polished for Jason's liking.

What does he want? Jason wondered as he strode forward to meet the man. Riding high on the back of a gleaming black gelding, Kellerman wore a black suit and flat-crowned hat. The lawyer's only tribute to his Western surroundings was his polished black boots.

"Good afternoon," Kellerman said. "I've come to see Miss Hastings."

Jason said, "She's inside. You can tie your horse here at the porch, unless you'd like me to take him to the barn."

"That won't be necessary. I won't be long." He dismounted and unfastened a leather case tied to his blanket roll behind the saddle. "I have a few papers for her to sign, and then I'll be on my way."

Jason led the way to the front door, opened it, and stepped inside.

In the bedroom, Sharon was sitting in the rocking chair beside Max's bed. She was smiling at something Max had said. Through the window, the afternoon sun shone on her and made her flaxen hair gleam like pure sunbeams.

When she saw Jason's scowl, her smile faded. "What is it,

Jason?" she asked.

"Mr. Kellerman's here to see you."

Edward Kellerman stepped forward, grinning and bowing like some kind of duke.

Sharon rose to meet him. "How nice to see you again," she said, offering him her hand.

He bowed over it. For a moment, Jason thought the man would kiss it—and her with no glove on, either.

Jason took two steps back and quietly closed the door. Nothing for him to do in there except fight the urge to punch Edward Kellerman's distinguished nose.

❧

Edward glanced through Max's open door. "I didn't know you had sickness here. How is he doing?"

"Better, thank the Lord," Sharon said. She hurried to the spare room door. "I'll close this, Max, so you can rest." He already had his eyes closed when she pulled it shut.

She turned to the lawyer. "Please, have a seat." She sat on the edge of the sofa. "What brings you to the ranch, Edward?" she asked when he found a place across from her.

"I have some papers for you to sign," he said, "but I'm in no hurry." He unbuttoned his jacket and leaned back. "How do you like the ranch?"

"It's massive," Sharon said. "Jason took me over part of it on Monday."

"Did you see the famous water hole?"

"Is it famous?"

"You'd be surprised." He picked up the leather case and rested it on his lap. "How are the hands treating you?"

Sharon smiled. "They already feel like family. At first I wasn't sure if I could make it here, but now I really want to try. I've got good people here. Leaving now would break my heart."

He nodded. "I'm glad to hear that." Leaning forward, he said, "Would you mind if I come to call on you sometime?"

Her heart lurched. Her cheeks grew warm. "That would be nice, Edward." How could her voice sound so calm? She swallowed and drew in a long, slow breath.

He unclasped the leather case. "The will has been sent to probate court in Albuquerque. Once it's recorded, the property can be sold. However, in the meanwhile, your uncle's wishes for maintaining the ranch are being carried out. It's going on as before." He paused to look into her eyes. "I want you to know that I'm totally at your service, Sharon. Anything you need—or even want—let me know and I'll take care of it."

"That's very kind," she said, "but there's nothing that I need at the moment."

He pulled some pages from the case and moved to sit beside her. His shoulder brushed hers as he leaned to point out where she should sign. "This is a document transferring the mortgage to your name as the new owner. As you can see there's a debt of $2,061.49 and a yearly payment of $463.32 due on October 1 every year."

Sharon took her time reading through the closely written script. The mortgage payment seemed huge. Just looking at the amount gave her a knot in her stomach. Finally, she said, "Should I pay a visit to the banker?"

"If you'd like to, you can do that, but it's not absolutely necessary. The banker's name is Tom Jenkins. He's a nice chap, a friend of mine."

Sharon looked up. "We'd better move to the table so I can set this down to write on it." She stood and walked five steps to the kitchen table.

Edward moved fast enough to pull out her chair for her. From his case he pulled a small bottle of ink, then filled a fountain pen and handed it to her. When she gave the pen back to him, he pulled a lever on its side to release the ink back into the bottle and wiped the tip with a small cloth. As he tucked the cloth into his case and slid the pen into a slot, he said, "How about next Saturday morning? Around ten o'clock? Not the Saturday coming, I mean, but the one after that."

Sharon stared at him, not sure what he was talking about.

He went on, "Would it be convenient for me to call on you then?"

She couldn't believe that she had already forgotten. "That would be fine," she said. "I'll look forward to it."

He bowed over her hand, said, "Good day," and left in short order.

He had no sooner closed the door when Lucy came from the middle bedroom. Her cheek still showed the marks from where she had been sleeping on the pillow.

Watching Sharon, Lucy giggled. "You may not know it, but you've got a date with the most eligible bachelor in the territory." She plopped into a chair at the table. "I can't believe it. You just got here, and you've already had two callers."

"I'm just a new face, that's all," Sharon replied. To get Lucy off the uncomfortable subject, Sharon hurried on, "Lucy, I have lots of clothes that I don't need. They would fit you perfectly. Would you be offended if I gave them to you? If you don't like any of them, you can give them to someone else."

"Offended?" Lucy demanded. She wrapped her arms around Sharon. "I haven't had a new dress since I was sixteen years old."

"Oh, these aren't new."

"They'll be new to me." She hugged Sharon again.

The girls went into Sharon's room to sort her things. Sharon emptied one of her trunks and happily stuffed it with everything from nightgowns to crinolines to silk dresses. Finally, they jammed the lid shut.

"Mother will think I'm awful for taking all this," Lucy said.

"You're doing me a favor," Sharon insisted. "I feel guilty having so much when you have so little. We'll get Wilson to put it on the wagon when he takes you home tonight."

Before retiring that evening, Sharon went to check on Max. For once, he didn't say anything when she came in.

She picked up his empty pitcher. "Do you need anything else?" she asked.

"Have a seat, Sharon." When she eased into the rocking chair, he went on. "Rudolph had a lot of faith in Stewart Pitt. Stewart was his lawyer for thirty-five years. After Stewart died, this young fellow Kellerman came to town and took up the law office. He's been in Farmington for nigh on two years." He gazed at her. "The way I hear it, since he came to town he has called on the banker's daughter, the mayor's daughter, and the daughters of four big ranchers."

Sharon laughed. "Don't look so worried. He asked me if he could come to call. He didn't propose." Still laughing, she took his dishes to the kitchen and slid them into the soapy water in the dishpan. Yet even as she laughed, a nagging doubt formed in her mind. Edward Kellerman was handsome and very smooth. Was that what she wanted in a man?

❦

After a week in bed, Max moved back into the bunkhouse. Sharon missed him. It had been nice to have someone else in the house in the evenings after Lucy went home. He was able to return to work on the last day of June.

The weather grew warmer by the day, and no rain came to break the heat. She helped Max set up a summer kitchen in the lean-to behind the house. That did a lot to ease the scorching afternoons.

After another downpour, it didn't rain for the next two weeks and the heat became relentless.

Sharon was scrubbing clothes in a big iron pot on a stand in the backyard when Wilson galloped his horse across the field. Normally, the men kept the horses to a moderate pace, so Sharon watched his arrival with concern. He went to the barn, dropped the reins, and strode inside.

A few minutes later Jason appeared in the barn door and headed for the house. Sharon waved at him and called, "I'm over here! What's wrong?" She had images of one of Corky's boys hurt or maybe a horse down. She dropped the skirt she was rubbing on the washboard and hurried to meet him.

His eyebrows were drawn together, his mouth tense. "Our neighbor to the south, Jared O'Bannon, has run his cattle to our water hole. He had to cut a fence to do it."

"Why would he do something like that?" Sharon asked.

"It hasn't rained for weeks, and things are getting dry farther south." Sharon's dismay must have shown on her face because his expression softened a little, so did his voice. "It's not a catastrophe at this point. There's plenty of water—more than enough for both of our cattle. But I'm going to have to find out why they're trespassing."

He went on, "O'Bannon's spread is called the Double O. He and his men usually keep to themselves. I'm going to ride over there and have a talk with his hands."

"I'm going with you," she said.

He tilted his head. "That's not necessary, Sharon. I can take care of it."

She dried her hands on her apron. "I'm not doubting you, Jason, but I want to go. I *am* going with you."

His face took on that guarded look again. "Suit yourself.

I'll saddle the horses."

On her way inside to change, she stopped in the kitchen to talk to Max for a moment. He was kneading bread dough on the counter when she stepped through the back door. He stopped working and turned toward her when she told him of Wilson's news.

"What kind of man is Jared O'Bannon?" she asked. "Has Uncle Rudolph had trouble with him before?"

Max leaned against the counter. His apron was smudged with flour and dabbed with grease. "No trouble," he said, "but O'Bannon can be hotheaded if you get on his wrong side. He almost had a feud going with the Box B a few years back. It was over a fence line, I believe. No shots were fired, but it was tough going for a while there.

"Rudolph fought shy of the man," he went on. "He said a man with a temper is worse than a gun with a hair trigger."

"I hope we don't have any trouble," Sharon said, moving toward her room.

"We?" Max called after her.

"I'm going with Jason to talk to those men," she said. Before he could answer, she latched the door firmly behind her.

She changed into a riding skirt and fresh blouse and recombed her hair. She had always felt a little out of her depth here, but she had a heavy responsibility to fulfill. Nothing was going to stop her. Not even a hotheaded range lord.

"Don't borrow trouble, girl," she told her image in the shadowy mirror above the washstand. "Wait until you meet the man. He might be all right."

She threw open the windows, glad the room had windows on three sides. Maybe it would cool off a little after dark. As much as she had hated the damp and chill of the June rain, she longed for it now.

She heard the horses outside and hurried to meet Jason.

Ignoring his stony face, she led out on Ginger, a high-spirited bay mare. Jason soon came up beside her and they road abreast for a while.

"Let's swing south and check the fence line!" he called. "We need to know what we're dealing with before we meet those hands."

When they reached the fence, Jason got down to take a closer look. Sharon joined him. "See that?" he asked, holding up a strand of loose wire. "This was definitely cut." He threw it down. "Who would be so brainless as to do a fool thing like that? Shooting wars have been started for less. A lot less."

"Well, now we know," she said, heading for her horse. "Let's go see what they have to say."

He swung up. "I doubt O'Bannon will be there himself. He may not even know what they're up to."

A few minutes later, the water hole came into view. Fifty longhorns drank from its rim while fifty more browsed the clumps of grass nearby. Double O brands mixed with the Lazy H cattle.

When the Double O hands caught sight of Jason and Sharon, they sat up straighter and stared. A tall, gangly cowboy on a black stallion rode toward them in a cloud of dust.

"That's Luther Heinburg, O'Bannon's foreman," Jason told Sharon.

Heinburg came close, then had to back away when the stallion reared his head back.

"What do you think you're doing, cutting our fence?" Sharon burst out before Jason could speak. "Do you want to start a shooting war right off or do you want to wait a day or two?"

Heinburg stared at her, then glanced at Jason.

"If you know what's good for you, you'll round them all up and move back to your own property," Sharon went on. "You're lucky I'm in a good mood today. I ought to call the law. There's a legal name for what you did."

O'Bannon's foreman glanced toward the three men behind him, then pinned her with a hard stare. "That's big talk from a girl with only one cowpoke to side her."

She gasped, truly angry now. "Are you threatening me on my own land?" She worked the reins as Ginger sidestepped and pranced. When the horse settled down, she went on. "Do you really think that I'd let all my men stand out here exposed? What's the range on a good rifle with a scope, do you think?"

Scanning the horizon, Heinburg's Adam's apple bobbed. He went on in a more reasonable tone. "Our groundwater is halfway down," he said. "We didn't think—"

"That's right. You didn't think," she said. "I suggest you begin to use your head, starting right now."

With another glance at Jason, Heinburg wheeled his horse and headed back to his men. After a short confab and several glances their way, the hands began the tedious process of separating out their cattle and herding them south.

Sharon noticed that Jason's ears were red. He had his jaw clamped down and didn't look at her.

When the Double O cows started moving, Jason ground out, "We may as well head out. They'll be here most of the day. Wilson and Corky will come back before dark and fix that fence." He wheeled his horse and set off at a leisurely trot.

She followed him until they were out of sight of the Double O hands. Then her hands started shaking like a willow tree in a windstorm. She felt sick to her stomach and a little faint.

She closed her eyes and drew in several calming breaths. At least Mrs. Minniver had taught her how to get control of herself.

Jason continued ahead, gaining distance by the minute.

She urged Ginger to catch up to him. "Hey, wait for me!" she called when she drew closer.

He ignored her, and her temper flared.

"What's the matter?" she demanded, coming up beside him. "They backed down."

He kept his face straight ahead. "Right. That's just what they did." He leaned forward and kicked his horse to a gallop. Sharon let him go. If he was that bad-tempered, she didn't want to talk to him anyway.

When she reached the ranch yard, Jason and Wilson were in a close conversation outside the barn door. Jason wore a scowl as Wilson spoke rapidly.

When Jason came to the house for dinner a few minutes later, a hint of that scowl remained.

"What happened out there?" Max asked when they began to eat. "What did O'Bannon say?"

"He wasn't there. It was his foreman," Sharon replied, scooping potatoes onto her plate. "I told him to gather up his cows and leave, and that's what he did." She set the bowl down and picked up a dish of peas.

"Jason?" Max prodded.

He drank coffee and didn't answer right away. Setting his cup down, he said, "Heinburg didn't know what to do when he had a woman facing him down. He couldn't pull a gun on her, could he?"

Chuckling, Max turned to Sharon. "You faced him down? Good for you."

She smiled at Max, then noticed that Wilson's lips were turned down, and Jason was glaring at his steak.

Sharon ignored them and focused her attention on her food. When she looked up, Jason was gone, finished before anyone else. Wilson left soon afterward.

"What did I do wrong?" she asked Max. "I went out there to protect my property. And that's what I did. Why is Jason so angry?"

The little man worked his lips left, then right, considering. "It's not what you did," he said. "It's what you did with Jason looking on. This is a man's world, Sharon. Jason was shamed because you took charge of the situation."

Her eyes flashed. "I may be a woman, but I'm also the owner of this ranch."

"And a good one," he told her. "You did fine, Sharon. Give the men a chance to simmer down, and they'll be all right."

After helping Max clear the table, she retired early. She had a sick feeling in her stomach and a distinct urge to cry.

Lying awake long after dark, she tried to figure out what had gone wrong that afternoon. The answer: nothing. Whatever the problem was, it was in the male mind of Jason Riordan.

She turned over and closed her eyes, willing herself to sleep. Tomorrow was Saturday. Edward would be coming to call in the morning, and she wanted to be up early. She had a lot to do. Press a dress, wash her hair. . . .

❧

Jason Riordan lay back on his bunk and stared at the pine boards on the ceiling. He flung his hands up to settle them behind his head. His thoughts wandered to Sharon's set-to with Luther Heinburg. Jason had seen red when she took over and faced Heinburg down herself. But now that he'd had time to cool off, he had to admire her nerve.

He chuckled softly. What a girl. Eighteen years old, on the range for no more than a month, and she was ready to take them all on. O'Bannon included. He'd never met a female like her in all his life.

Bringing one arm forward to cover his eyes, he fell asleep with the hint of a smile still on his face.

eight

A few minutes after ten o'clock, Edward arrived on his black gelding. Sharon went out to meet him. She had chosen a navy dress in soft calico with a tiny strip of lace around the neck.

"Good morning," he said, ground-hitching his horse in the grass under the big tree in the front yard. "All right if I leave Midnight here?"

"Will he be happier there or in the barn?" she asked.

"He's in the shade, and there's plenty of grass. He'll be fine."

She paused beside the door, waiting for him to reach her. "Would you like some coffee?"

"In this heat? A cool glass of water sounds more like it." He removed his hat as he crossed the threshold and followed Sharon into the kitchen.

She pumped the handle of the pitcher pump four times to prime it, and water gushed out into the metal pitcher standing there.

"Max is in the corral, training a yearling," she said, pouring water into a glass. "Would you like to watch him for while?" She handed it to Edward.

He took a long drink, then said, "Actually, I'd like to sit on the porch for a spell, if you don't mind. We can enjoy the breeze and talk."

"That sounds wonderful," she said. Actually, she'd rather go to the corral, but she could do that any time.

Sitting close together on the short bench, they talked about the need for rain while they watched Midnight leisurely cropping grass. When conversation ran thin, Sharon said, "Would you like to go for ride? It's cooler out by the water hole."

He made his little bow. "Your wish is my command."

She stood. "Would you ask Wilson to saddle Ginger for me? It'll take a minute for me to change." She hurried to her room and got into her riding clothes, which were waiting on the peg behind the door.

When she reached the barn, the black barn cat and her kittens were sunning themselves at the edge of the doorway. "Hello, kitties," Sharon said, wishing she could pet them. The next litter, she'd be there to tame the kittens before they got so big and wild.

Inside, she found Edward watching Wilson tightening the cinch strap around Ginger, a tall bay mare with a black tail and a white blaze on her face. Wilson looked up when Sharon approached, concern on his grizzled face.

"Are you sure you want Ginger?" he asked. "She can be tetchy."

"I rode her yesterday," Sharon replied. "We'll get along fine." She stroked the mare's neck. "Won't we, Ginger?" The mare nickered and nuzzled Sharon's blouse.

Wilson slipped the bit into the horse's mouth and fit the headstall over her head. "If you say so," he said doubtfully. He glanced at Edward, then continued speaking to Sharon. "I reckon you'll have help if you need it."

Sharon gathered the reins and led the horse to the mounting block. "We're only going to the water hole and back. We should be gone an hour or two at the most."

Wilson nodded but didn't reply.

Edward said, "I'll fetch Midnight," and strode out the open double doors.

As Sharon slid into the saddle, Jason ambled in through the door leading to the corral. His chin came up an inch or two when he caught sight of Edward's back going through the barn door. "Going riding?" he asked when he reached Sharon.

"I thought we'd ride to the water hole. I want to see how the Double O people left it. Besides, it's cooler out there." Why did she feel defensive?

His lips twisted. "What brought Kellerman out here so soon? More papers to sign?"

Looking down at him, she didn't like the way his eyebrows slanted as he waited for her reply.

Not answering him was a direct violation of Rule 4. With her face muscles under strict control, her gaze toward the distance, she nudged Ginger. The mare's hoofbeats echoed and reverberated through the posts and beams of the massive structure. Sitting astride Midnight, Edward met her at the door, and they set off at a canter.

Riding at that pace made conversation impossible. She savored the sage-scented air and focused on the movements of the horse beneath her, the lazy looping of a hawk overhead, and the feeling of the wind on her face.

When they stopped to give the horses a rest, Sharon told Edward about the Double O hands and their cattle at the water hole. Intent on her words, he drew his horse closer. His face had smooth planes. His eyes were wide-set and dark. He was the most handsome man Sharon had ever known.

"So, you let them turn around and go home? That's it?" he asked.

Her eyes narrowed. "What are you trying to say?"

He drew back a little. "I wonder if you shouldn't let the sheriff know what's going on. For your own protection, Sharon. In a situation like this, things can get out of hand in a heartbeat."

"I'll think about that," she told him. "I don't want to make the situation worse by calling in the law. Max said he thinks they were trying to see how far I can be pushed, being the new owner and new to the area. I'm hoping he's right and they won't try anything again."

"As long as it rains before too long, you'll be all right," Edward replied. "If this drought gets worse, all bets are off."

Tired of the conversation, she squeezed her knees into the mare's sides and Ginger lurched ahead. Both woman and horse enjoyed a good run. Sharon let the mare have her head for a few minutes, then reined her in.

Edward caught up to them in seconds. He was grinning. "That horse has a lot of pep," he said. "Wilson was right."

"I can handle her." Sharon leaned over to speak to the horse. "Good girl, Ginger. You and I are going to be best friends."

"Let's walk awhile," Edward suggested a few minutes later.

"The water hole is over there," Sharon told him, urging Ginger ahead.

They soon reached the water's edge, and Edward helped her down—not that she really needed help. His hands lingered in hers. Uncomfortable, she turned away to walk along the bank.

The next moment, she drew up, alarmed. The water level was about a foot lower than its original depth. "Look how low it is!" she cried. "What will we do if it dries up?"

"Say, that sounds like you're borrowing grief that will most likely never happen." He took her hand and placed it inside his elbow. "Let's forget about the drought and walk for a while."

The gentle breeze was cooler here than at the ranch. Sharon had a sudden urge to bring a bedroll and bunk down here instead of on that sweltering straw tick that Rudolph had called a bed.

"So tell me," Edward said as they strolled along the bank, "what are your plans?"

"Plans?" She tried to think. "Well, tomorrow I'm taking Sunday dinner at Lucy's house. I was supposed to go long ago, but then Max got sick and other things got in the way. Finally, I'm going to be able to go. After that, I'm not sure."

"Would you ever consider selling the ranch? If you had a good offer?"

She laughed. "Do you know anyone with a million dollars? That's my best price."

He chuckled. "Not offhand. I'll let you know if I come across anyone though."

"Be sure you do."

At that moment the faint cry of an animal came from a nearby stand of mesquite. "Is that a sheep?" Sharon asked.

Edward turned around. "Where?"

The cry came again.

Sharon pointed toward the brush. "Over there. It sounds like a sheep." Pulling away from him, she crossed twenty yards of hard-packed earth. When she reached the mesquite, she gasped. Before her lay a mother goat that had been torn by some animal. Beside the dead mother stood a small she-kid about a month or two old. The baby backed away from Sharon but stayed nearby.

"I wonder if she's weaned," Sharon said, stooping down and watching the kid. It had a black body with a black face and tiny white hooves.

"It must have been a bobcat or a coyote," Edward said, still looking at the mother goat. "It's strange that whatever it was got the mother and left the kid."

"The kid may have been sleeping under some brush."

"Did Rudolph keep goats?" Edward asked.

"Max has two nannies that he milks," Sharon said. "I don't

know of any others. I'll have to ask." The kid took two steps toward its mother. Its little pointed chin quivered when it bawled.

"We can't leave the baby here for another wild animal to find," Sharon said. "I couldn't sleep knowing it was out here."

Edward stared down at his pressed black suit and glanced at the bawling kid.

"It should be easy to catch her," Sharon told him. "Circle around and move in. The kid will forget about me and run for her mother. I'll get her when she gets close enough."

And that's exactly how it worked. The problem was figuring out what to do with a wriggling baby goat once you caught it.

"I was going to hold it and carry it home," Sharon said, arching her head back as she clutched the thrashing kid, "but it will annoy the horse with all this kicking."

Edward said, "How about if we wrap it in a saddle blanket? I always carry one for emergencies."

"Hurry! I'm losing my grip!"

He pulled loose the two rawhide thongs holding the wool blanket roll behind his saddle and flipped the blanket open. Holding it with his arms apart, he came to Sharon and wrapped his arms around the kid. Sharon had trouble pulling her arms away with Edward holding the kid so tightly. Their cheeks touched, and she felt the roughness of his sideburn against her face.

Finally, she was able to take a step back.

"Wrap the blanket around her a few times," he said, "so she can't move."

Sharon wrapped her up in short order. Only her black ears and glistening black eyes were able to move. Sharon took the rawhide strings from Edward's hand and tied the blanket around the kid's hind feet and front feet, making her sharp hooves harmless.

"Put her across my saddle," she said. "I'll carry her home."

Once the horse began to move, the kid settled down. Sharon kept her hand against the blanket roll, so she wouldn't slip off the saddle. "What are we going to name you?" she asked the tiny bundle. "Emily? Sarah?"

"Did you say something?" Edward called.

"I'm trying to figure out what to call her," Sharon told him. "Any suggestions?"

He didn't answer.

"Sophie!" she cried. Stroking the kid's ears, she cooed, "Your name is Sophie. Little Sophie, baby girl."

By the time they reached the house, Max was setting lunch on the table. "What in the world?" he exclaimed when he saw the bundle in Sharon's arms.

"It's a baby goat," Sharon told him. "Something got her mother. We found her by the water hole."

"Bring her back to the nanny pen, and we'll see if one of them will feed her. If not. . ." He shook his head.

Edward spoke from the doorway. "Sharon, I've got to be going. I'll see you tomorrow in church."

Sharon jerked around. She'd forgotten Edward. Where were her manners? "Edward, I'm so sorry! I'm afraid I've spoiled your morning."

"Not at all. I have an appointment this afternoon, and I must be on my way."

Still holding Sophie, she called, "Thanks for coming!"

He turned away from the door, and she rushed to follow Max. The poor baby had to be roasting in that blanket. She had to get her unwound right away.

The nanny pen was fifty feet from the back door, a room-sized area with a small structure at the back for protection from the elements. Inside its shade, two gray goats with small curved horns lay resting. Farther back in the yard, another pen held five or six more goats.

"Give me the bundle," Max said holding out his arms. He took the baby inside and shut the gate behind him. He set the kid down and pulled loose the rawhide strings. Soon, the baby stood swaying and crying in the center of the yard. Immediately both nannies stood up and started bawling. One nanny came close, raised her nose, and sniffed the air, then turned away. The other nanny came up to the kid and nuzzled her. The kid trotted around and began to nurse.

Max beamed. "That one lost a kid a couple of months back. Rubbing his bald head, he let himself out of the pen. "I wasn't sure it would work. You never know."

"Her name is Sophie," Sharon said. "She's the first thing on this ranch that's really mine."

Max came to stand beside her. He leaned his arms against the top fence rail to watch the new baby. "What was it like living at that boarding school?" he asked.

A sudden rush of a deep sadness made it hard for Sharon to speak. "I cried for Mama every night for the first year. After that, all I thought about was coming here."

Max moved closer to her. Together, they watched the baby and its adopted mother for a few more minutes.

Finally, Max said, "The men will be coming up for lunch. I'd best put food on the table."

"I need to wash up," Sharon said, falling into step with him.

"Your gentleman friend took out for home, I guess."

"He said he had an appointment," Sharon said.

"He must be dedicated. First lawyer I ever heard of that keeps hours on Saturday afternoon." Max stomped up the two steps to the back door. He pumped water into a basin, so she could wash her hands.

Jason and Wilson arrived a few minutes later.

"We found an orphan kid at the water hole," Sharon told him, lifting a towel from a nail nearby. "A bobcat or maybe a wolf got its mother. I brought it home, and Max put it in the nanny pen."

"How did a goat and a kid get there?" He turned to Wilson behind him. "Do we have any goats on the range?"

Wilson had a creaky voice with a hint of whine in it. "It could have wandered over here from the reservation. There's no way of telling really. . .unless the Double O has taken to branding everything that moves."

The men chuckled at that and took their seats, anxious to dig into thick beef sandwiches and hearty vegetable soup.

"Didn't your boyfriend stay for lunch?" Jason joked to Sharon.

"First of all, he's my lawyer," she shot back. "And second, he had business to attend to." She made a point of turning toward Max. "I'm going to eat with the Riordan family tomorrow after church, so it'll only be you and Wilson for lunch," she said.

Max glanced toward Wilson. "It's not often you get to call the menu," he told the cowhand. "Now's your chance. Give it your best shot."

❧

Sharon spent most of the afternoon hovering around the nanny pen. When Max came out to milk the goats that evening, he said, "Why don't you come inside with me? They won't hurt you."

The nursing nanny was standing on the opposite side of the pen with Sophie beside her. The second nanny stood in the lean-to.

Sharon said, "When I was about six, a goat knocked me down. I've been wary of them ever since."

"These girls are harmless," he said, swinging the gate open for her to enter ahead of him. He set down the stool and bucket he was carrying. Gripping the collar of the non-nursing goat, he led her to a short rope hanging from the fence and tied her there. "I'll leave the other one to nurse your baby," he said. "From the size of that kid, she should be weaned in a couple of weeks."

Sharon edged up to the kid and held out her hand for Sophie to sniff. To her delight, the kid let Sharon stroke her head. "Sophie," she crooned. "You're a sweetie." The next thing she knew, Max was gone, and she was in the pen alone.

She stayed until the triangle jangled for dinnertime.

nine

The next morning, Sharon was up at first light. She threw on an old housedress and hurried to the nanny pen to check on Sophie. Today, Sharon would stay at the Riordans' cabin after church, so she wouldn't see Sophie again until late afternoon.

The baby goat was lying contentedly next to her new mama. Satisfied that she was okay, Sharon went to the cooking lean-to to give Max a hand. She pulled an apron from a peg and tied it around her waist. "Jason will be delighted to see hotcakes for breakfast," she told him. "Do you want me to fry the bacon?"

"How are you at turning hotcakes?" he asked. "I never have cottoned to that part of it. I always feel like every hotcake is a personal test, and I can't pass every time."

"I can't promise that I will, either," Sharon told him with a small laugh. "But I love a challenge."

He handed her the wide spatula and moved aside. A long iron grill covered two burners on the hot stove. The yellow crockery bowl stood nearby, full of yellow frothy batter and a small ladle. Max moved to the other side of the stove and filled a hot skillet with thick-cut bacon. On the short counter behind them lay a large bowl of peeled potatoes in water, and beside it a head of cabbage and a bowl of string beans.

After breakfast Sharon's cheeks were still rosy from the heat as she went to change for church. She'd only worn the navy calico dress for a few minutes yesterday, so she'd wear it again this morning. She spent extra time on her hair to form a deep wave over the right side of her forehead. Her arms ached before she was satisfied, but she finally got it right.

Jason was already on the porch when she stepped outside. He helped her into the buckboard and set off at a nice clip.

"I wish this wagon had a roof like the surrey," she said. "If it's this hot now, what will it be like after church?"

"Just wait until we get inside the building," Jason remarked dryly. "I hope the parson is as hot and anxious to get outside as the rest of us."

Rev. Nelson, however, was oblivious to the weather and kept them until a few minutes to one. Sharon could hardly wait to get to the cabin. Even with a cotton dress, she was much too warm.

"Ma can hardly wait to meet you," Lucy said when they set off from the church. "She's been talking about it all week."

The Riordan cabin was basically one large room. The fireplace covered the east wall. A settee, two chairs, and a heavily padded rocking chair stood in a semicircle before it. On the rear wall were two narrow doors.

On the other side of the room, the kitchen area resembled the one at the main ranch house, except it was half the size of Max's domain. A stairs at the back of the kitchen told that there was a second floor under the eaves of the roof. The house smelled of coal oil and liniment. The floor was worn in places and the covering on the settee was frayed, but it felt like a house filled with happy memories, strong faith, and lots of love.

When they came in, Mrs. Riordan was sitting in the rocking chair beside the cold fireplace. Her face was thin and deeply etched from years of constant pain. In her younger days, she must have been a beauty like Lucy. Now her hair was white, her eyes two dark hollows in her pale face.

Lucy bent over to kiss her mother's cheek. "Ma, meet Sharon Hastings."

Sharon drew near and gently clasped the woman's gnarled hand. She knelt to be at eye level with her. "Mrs. Riordan, I've been looking forward to meeting you. I have so much to thank you for. If not for Uncle Rudolph's generosity and your kindness, I don't know what would have happened to me."

As she gazed into the older woman's eyes, Sharon had the urge to cry. If there was ever a loving mother, this was her.

Resting her hand on Sharon's head, Mrs. Riordan said, "Give thanks to God, child. He's the One who gives perfect gifts." She opened her arms and drew Sharon to her breast.

Tears flowed down Sharon's cheeks. She felt embarrassed, but she couldn't stop them. Her broken heart had yearned for this moment ever since she had lost her mother.

When she drew back, Mrs. Riordan's cheeks were wet, too.

Jason pulled a chair closer, and Sharon sank into it. She took out her handkerchief and tried to dry her streaming eyes.

"Tell me about your parents," Mrs. Riordan said, dabbing at her own cheeks.

Sharon swallowed and forced her voice to work. "Mama was the best cook in our neighborhood when we lived in Missouri." She sniffed and pressed her handkerchief against her nose. "I didn't appreciate it back then, but after I got to boarding school. . ." Her throat closed up, and she couldn't speak for a moment.

Finally, she drew in a quavering breath. "She loved planting flowers. She took a dozen cuttings with her on the Oregon Trail." She talked on without stopping until Lucy called them to the table. It felt so good to be able to talk about those she loved. She hadn't been able to until now.

"I'm sorry, Mrs. Riordan," Sharon said as they stood. "I've been rattling on and on and boring you unmercifully."

"Not in the least, my dear," the older woman said as Jason helped her move to the table. "I've been waiting for five long years to get to know you. I expect you to come and talk to me regularly."

"I will," Sharon said. How could she stay away?

After Jason prayed, Lucy passed Sharon a platter of fried chicken and told her mother, "Sharon has a new baby, an orphan she found yesterday."

"You don't say," Mrs. Riordan said with a feeble smile. "And what kind of baby is it, Sharon?"

"It's a tiny black goat about six weeks old. Its mother was killed by a wild animal. I couldn't bear to leave her to die, so I brought her home and named her Sophie. One of our milking nannies has adopted her. She's doing quite well."

"You named her?" Jason asked, amused.

"And why not? She's the first thing on the Lazy H that's really mine, and I intend to treat her special."

Jason laughed. "The men will enjoy that," he said. He slanted his eyes at his sister. "Life is going to be different with a lady running things around there. I can see that right now."

"I, for one, am glad," Lucy declared, smiling at Sharon.

Sharon turned to Jason. "In all the excitement yesterday, I forgot to tell you that the water hole is a foot down."

He laid down his fork. "I know. I was out there two days ago. I can't imagine what the ranchers south of here must be dealing with." He looked at his mother. "We need to have special prayer for rain, Ma. Things are getting critical."

"I have been praying, son," she said. "The Good Lord knows what He's doing. Even if we can't figure Him out."

After the meal, Mrs. Riordan announced that she must lie down, and Lucy went to help her. Feeling that it was time to give them privacy, Sharon said good-bye to both ladies.

"I can walk home if you want to stay awhile," she told Jason when they were alone.

"No reason for that," he said shortly. "I've got some things to see to this afternoon. I was planning to go back to the ranch anyway."

He held the door for her and then helped her into the buckboard.

As they jostled down the trail, Sharon said, "I'd like to go into town sometime this week. I need a few things."

"Talk to Max," he said. "I know he'd be glad to go along. He's always needing something for the kitchen." He leaned toward her with a conspiratorial air. "Tell him to get some of that fine sugar to dust on doughnuts. We haven't had them for coon's age."

She let her mouth fall open for a second. "Jason Riordan, you have a sweet tooth!"

He chuckled. "That being my only weakness, I think I'm doing all right."

She laughed aloud.

Not wanting to lose the moment, she asked, "Have you always wanted to be foreman of the Lazy H? Didn't you ever dream of doing something else?"

He shifted his legs and found a more comfortable position on the seat. Tilting his head back, he thought about that. "I can't say I ever did. I started mucking out the stalls when I was eleven or twelve years old. After that, there was always something to keep me busy. I never had a lot of time to think of leaving or doing something else. Everything I wanted was here."

He glanced in her direction. "That must seem pretty tame to you. You've been over half the country and back again."

"Not that it did me much good," she replied. "Believe me, there's nothing out there that you don't have right here."

Though he didn't move an inch, his look became somehow closer and more intent. "Now that you're here," he murmured, "I reckon that's true."

ten

Monday morning, while helping Max in the kitchen, Sharon said, "I'd like to go into town sometime this week. Do you think you could find time to go with me?"

He stopped pinching off biscuits. Covered in clumps of flour, his hands hovered over the baking pan. "That's a grand idea. I need some things."

She grinned. "Jason told me you'd say that." She told him Jason's request for sugar-sprinkled doughnuts.

"Ha! I'm not surprised." He pinched off an egg-sized lump of dough and dropped it onto the baking pan. "That boy would eat sweets the livelong day." He finished the last bit of dough and rubbed his hands over the bowl to clear them off. "How about tomorrow?" he asked.

"Let's eat at a restaurant. My treat."

With Max driving the surrey, they set off for town around nine o'clock on Tuesday morning. She had chosen the pink gingham dress today because it was cooler than most of her others. Its bonnet was of matching gingham lined with white muslin. She carried her white cotton gloves in her purse until they reached town. No sense soiling them on the ride in.

Wearing a cream-colored Stetson and a blue chambray shirt with a black string tie, Max looked fine. He had to sit on the edge of the seat to reach the brake.

"Are you from Farmington originally?" Sharon asked him.

"I was born in Santa Fe. I had a good business there when I was only twenty-one years old. I had almost two hundred people under me."

Sharon gasped. "And you gave it up to be a cook?"

He laughed, too tickled to answer right away. "I—I mowed a graveyard."

It took a moment for her to understand. Then she laughed. "Max, you are too much."

"Seriously, I came north to run cows in the early seventies. I stayed in this corner of the territory, working for one rancher or another. I was in Farmington between jobs when I got the word that the Lazy H was looking for a cook. I've always been a hand in the kitchen, so I came out and took the job. Breaking horses is a hobby. No one ever told me I had to do it. I just do."

"I'm glad you're at the ranch, Max. You've made things so much easier for me."

He patted her hand. "Same here, my dear. I don't know what would have become of me if you hadn't been there while I was sick." He sighed. "It's such a shame about Rudolph. I can't get over it. He wasn't a young man, but he was still in his prime, full of life with plans for the future."

He glanced at her. "You were a big part of those plans, Sharon. He talked about you coming and what he wanted to do when you got here." He gazed into the distance. "Then one day, nothing. He was gone."

"I'm sorry I missed the funeral," she said.

"Funeral? There wasn't one. A few days before you came, we had a little private service at the house in his memory. The parson came, and we gathered in the living room. He read some verses and prayed. That was it."

He wiped his face with his handkerchief. Sharon did the same with hers. The heat was almost unbearable. Even in the shade of the surrey's roof, the top of her head felt the ruthless rays of the blistering sun.

When they reached town, Sharon pulled on her gloves and

said, "Let's go to the bank first. I want to meet Tom Jenkins."

Max nodded. "I know him. Good man. Rudolph liked him." He angled the wagon to the edge of the street and jumped down. Moving quickly, he looped the reins around the hitching rail, then came to help her down.

The Farmington National Bank was an unpainted structure in the center of the main street. It had double front doors with nine glass panes in each one. A bell jangled when they let themselves in.

Before them, a short counter had iron bars from its wooden top to the ceiling. A short, round man with black hair and a gray beard stood behind the counter.

"May I help you folks?" he asked.

Sharon said, "I'd like to see Tom Jenkins, if I may."

"Yes, miss. I'll tell him you're here." He disappeared through the door behind him for an instant. "He'll be right with you."

A minute later, the banker stepped out and came through a hinged half door at the end of the counter. He was built like a bear from his shape and size to his brown hair and dark eyes. When he saw Max, he beamed. "Well, Max Martin. It's good to see you."

"Tom, this is Sharon Hastings. Rudolph's niece."

She offered him her hand. "It's good to meet you, Mr. Jenkins. I've come to talk about the mortgage on the ranch."

Jenkins stood aside and held the half door open. "Please come into my office."

Max hesitated. "If it's all right with you, Sharon, I've got some things to attend to in town."

"Of course," Sharon replied. "I'll meet you at the general store."

Max trundled away.

Turning toward the banker, Sharon said, "I don't know

what we would do without Max."

Jenkins smiled down at her. "A man of many talents, to be sure."

The banker's office was much like Edward Kellerman's except it was triple in size and smelled of nasty cigars. The large open window behind the desk showed a dusty backyard with a cactus garden in one corner. The grass was brown and parched. The breeze coming through the window felt hot and dry.

Jenkins held the padded back of a leather chair until she took a seat, then sat down and waited for her to begin.

"There's no problem," she began. "I came to learn more about the terms of our mortgage and what's required of me as the new owner."

Jenkins leaned back, one elbow resting on the leather-covered chair arm. "I sent the paperwork over to Edward Kellerman," he said.

"Yes, he brought it to me to sign. Unfortunately, I didn't understand the terms. I was wondering if you could explain them to me."

"It's pretty straightforward. We financed the ranch fifteen years ago for six thousand dollars at 2 percent interest. Since that time, Rudolph Hastings has refinanced several times. At this date the full amount. . ." He leaned forward to open a huge volume. It was about half the size of that bottom step Wilson had repaired and twice as thick.

Running his finger down a long column of tiny writing, he paused, then said, "Is $2,061.49 with a single payment of $463.32 due once annually."

"Mr. Jenkins, what if we can't make that mortgage payment in October? If the drought continues much longer, we may not have any cattle to sell."

He nodded, his face grave. "Every other rancher in this

area has the same question on his mind, Miss Hastings. We understand that." He closed the book and shoved it farther back on the wide desk. "If you come up short, let me know, and we'll refinance for $2,524.81. Your new payment will be a few dollars more the following year, but that's unavoidable."

"I see." It was a short-term fix that left her with a bigger long-term problem.

"Is there anything else I can help you with?" he asked.

"No. That answered my question. Thank you." She stood and offered him her hand. "It's been a pleasure meeting you, Mr. Jenkins."

He gently squeezed her hand and let it fall. "The pleasure is mine, Miss Hastings. Feel free to stop in any time." He walked with her to the office doorway, and the teller opened the half door to let her out.

Closing the jangling bank door behind her, Sharon paused on the boardwalk, blinking in the brilliant glare. She waited for a wagon to pass, then crossed the street to the general store.

The store had both doors open like the mouth of an enormous barrel with its contents spilling out over the boardwalk—small kegs of nails and screws, a table piled high with hand tools and neatly wound lengths of rope, and a bare wooden table that the young clerk, Timothy Ingles, was filling with stacks of enamel dishes.

When he saw Sharon, he grinned and his whole face lit up. He had a wide smile and twinkling blue eyes, a boyish pug nose with a few freckles scattered across it.

"We had vegetables on here earlier," he told Sharon, "but we had to take them in. The sun is too hot, you know."

"It is too hot," Sharon agreed. "For people as well."

She noticed a ripe tomato on the windowsill and pointed to it. "You forgot one."

He shook his head. "That's for good luck," he said, still stacking plates. "A tomato on the windowsill keeps out bad luck. Didn't you know that?" He grinned again.

Setting the last stack of bowls on the table, he picked up the empty crate and followed her into the store.

"What can I get for you today?" he asked.

"I have a list here." She drew it out of her purse and gave it to him. "While you're filling that, I'd like to look around, if I may. This is my first time in the store."

"That's fine, Sharon," he said. "Take your time."

She spent the next half hour in the tiny shop. It had a narrow counter that wound around the three inner walls. Beneath the counter, more shelves contained everything from building tools to canned goods, eggbeaters, and coffee grinders. Wooden shelves lined the walls behind the counters, as well—from dress goods to ready-made shirts, ammunition, and so much more.

The front of the store had a wide variety of leather products for horses—two saddles, several bridles, quirts, and horse blankets—all in neat rows.

She picked up a pair of riding gloves and met Timothy at the counter. Handing the gloves to him, she said, "Max Martin, our cook, will be here soon. He'll have a list of things as well. Could you wrap up all of this and have it ready in about an hour?"

"Why, sure thing, Sharon," he said. He paused. "Uh, Sharon, would you mind if I ask you something?"

She waited, smiling softly to encourage him.

"Would you like to go riding with me up to Chimney Rock? The view up there will take your breath away."

"Why, that's a fine idea," she said, delighted at a chance to go on a riding excursion. "I'd love to see it."

"I have Saturday off. I'll come to fetch you."

"I'll pack a picnic lunch," she said, pleased.

At that moment, Max arrived, red-faced and puffing. He glanced from Sharon's smile to Timothy's delighted grin. "Sorry I'm late," he panted. "I went down to the livery stable to check on something and lost track of time."

"I'm in no hurry," Sharon told him. "Do you need to go anywhere else?"

He shook his head. Digging into his shirt pocket, he handed Timothy a short list.

A portly, middle-aged man with heavy jowls came through the back door. "Hello, Zach," Max said. "Have you met Rudolph's niece, Sharon Hastings?" He turned to Sharon. "This is Zach Ingles, the owner of the store. Timothy's father."

Zach Ingles smiled, and the shape of his face changed. "I'm proud to know you, Miss Hastings," he said, coming to shake her hand. "I hope you'll be happy in these parts."

"Why, thank you, Mr. Ingles," she said. "I'm sure I will."

Max and the storekeeper discussed the weather and the danger of drought to the cattlemen. Finally, the men said good-bye. Max and Sharon headed for the boardwalk.

"Let's eat lunch," Sharon said when they reached the doorway.

Max mopped his streaming face. "I'm all for that."

"Lead the way," she told him. "I've no idea where we are going." She waved to Timothy who had moved to a ladder some distance away.

When they reached the boardwalk, Max said, "Did you know that Rudolph used to have partial ownership in that store?"

"Jason mentioned that Uncle Rudolph had helped him get started. He didn't tell me he was a partial owner."

Max's large head bobbed. "He sold out to Ingles a few months back."

"Was there some kind of trouble?"

He shrugged. "Rudolph never discussed his business dealings. I have no idea what happened. You'd have to ask Zach Ingles about that."

The hotel was four doors down the street, a two-story structure that looked more like a large home than a public building. It had whitewashed siding and a large, wraparound porch that was half-filled with hungry patrons sitting at long, narrow tables.

The restaurant was bustling inside as well. People filled six more tables, and two young girls rushed around serving them. A small blond girl paused long enough to tell them, "We can serve you if you don't mind sitting on the porch. Today's meal is on there." She pointed to a blackboard nailed to the wall beside the door and hurried away.

Scrawled in white chalk was the following menu: ROAST BEEF, MASHED POTATOES, CARROTS, AND CORN: FIFTY CENTS.

When she passed their way again, Max raised two fingers toward the waitress. She nodded and dashed toward the kitchen.

On their way outside, they passed two cowboys going in.

"Is it always this busy here?" Sharon asked.

He nodded. "Evenings it's worse, especially when the stage is in."

Sinking onto a bench she said, "I'm glad we can sit out here. It's stifling inside."

"Kitchen heat," he said. "I don't know how the cook stands it all day. I may know how to cook, but working in that setup isn't my idea of a good life."

They sat in silence for a few minutes, nodding to people passing in or out.

Finally, Max said, "Did I hear you making a date with Zach Ingles' boy?"

She laughed. "It's not a date. We're going to ride up to Chimney Rock and see the view."

He chuckled. "That's not a date? Chimney Rock is one of the favorite haunts of the young people hereabouts."

She acted offended. "Well, this time it's not romance. I love to ride, and he offered to show me a new place, that's all."

"Maybe to you it is," Max said sagely as their food arrived.

❧

Two days passed and still no rain. By Thursday, the thought on everyone's mind was rain. The constant topic of conversation was rain. The prayer at every meal and every quiet moment was for rain.

Sharon's concern grew by the hour. What if the water hole dried up?

Max became conservative with the pump water in the kitchen. "If the water table is that low," he told her, "we could lose the prime on this pump and then we'll be carrying water from the pump in the yard—as long as that one holds up." He rubbed his shiny head. "The first year I was here, we had a terrible bad drought. I wouldn't want to live through that again."

eleven

Sharon found peace in her time with Sophie. Soon the kid was coming to the gate whenever Sharon arrived. She found a piece of red grosgrain ribbon and tied it around Sophie's neck. It was soft, so it wouldn't chafe her skin, yet strong enough so that it wouldn't break. The ribbon collar gave Sharon a handhold when she needed to control the kid.

Sophie was a lively baby. She bounced around the nanny pen from morning 'til night, only stopping to nurse or to nuzzle Sharon. By standing at the corner of her bedroom window, wedged against the headboard, Sharon could see the pen and watch Sophie's antics.

On Saturday morning Timothy Ingles rode in shortly after breakfast. He was at the door before Sharon realized he had arrived. She was sweeping out the doorway when he stepped onto the porch.

"Come in," she said, smiling.

He stared at her broom.

She eyed it to see what was wrong with it. Nothing she could tell.

"You should sweep *into* the house," he said. "Sweeping out is bad luck."

Moving to the porch, she swept the dirt off the edge, then turned to him. "I was about to check on Sophie, my goat. Would you like to come along?"

He nodded. "I brought along my pup. I hope you don't mind. He goes with me almost everywhere."

"Did you really? I've half a mind to bring Sophie along,

too. She follows me all over. I know she'll spend the day bawling until I get back." She led him through the house to the back door.

When they reached the pen, Sophie came to the gate, and Sharon laughed. "See what I mean?" She stroked the kid's black head.

Timothy said, "My pup grew up around all kinds of animals—goats, sheep, chickens, you name it. Let's see how they get along. Maybe you can bring her."

Sharon moved down the fence and untied a length of rope. "I've been keeping her on this when she's out, so I can bring her back to the pen when I'm ready. Otherwise, she'll run and run and run, and I'll have to wait until she gets hungry before I can put her back in." She leaned over to talk directly to Sophie. "You need to learn some manners, don't you, baby?" She tied the rope to the ribbon around the kid's neck and opened the gate.

Sophie bounded out. Sharon wound the end of the rope around her hand to keep it from slipping out of her grasp.

Timothy laughed. "She must be half jackrabbit."

"I don't know where she gets so much energy." Sharon's arm waved back and forth from Sophie's pulling. "She wears me out in half an hour, but she can keep doing this all day long."

They worked their way around the house. Timothy's mount was a golden-haired pony. He had his nose deep into the water trough when Sharon first saw him. A long-haired sheepdog lay nearby. When Timothy came around the corner, the dog stood up and wagged his feathery tail.

The young man patted his pant leg. "Here, Bandit."

The dog trotted over. He raised his nose to sniff Sophie, then politely ignored her.

"See what I mean?" he asked. "I think they'll be all right.

Go ahead and bring her along."

"If she gets tired before we get back, I'll put her across the saddle and carry her." Sharon tugged at the dancing rope. "I need to fetch my bonnet and our lunch basket. I'll be just a minute." She quickly tied Sophie's rope to the porch post and hurried inside.

When she came back, Corky had Ginger at the door, and they set off with Bandit roaming the countryside along the trail and Sophie bounding beside the horse.

"It's cooler in the mountains," Timothy said. "Once you get up there, you won't want to come back, I promise you."

"That I can believe," Sharon said. "I don't think I've ever seen a place so hot and dry in my life."

He pulled his horse up so they could ride side by side. "Where are you from?" he asked. "Back East?"

"Well, farther east than here. Missouri." She told him about her family and the boarding school.

"Tough luck for a kid," he said. "My ma died four years ago when I was twenty. That was hard enough. I can't imagine what it must have been like for you, losing your family at such a young age."

"I had friends at school. And I had Uncle Rudolph."

The trail stretched out long and flat before them. Ginger bobbed her head and Sharon laughed. "She wants to run." She patted the mare's neck. "Save it, girl. You'll get plenty of action before this day is out." She turned to Timothy. "I understand that my uncle and your father were partners at one time."

He nodded. "Rudolph was like a part of our family. He put up the first stake for Pa to start the store. He kept the books until I got old enough to learn it."

"Why did he sell his share? It seems strange when the store is doing so well."

"I'm not really sure. He said that he had enough on his mind with his ranching and he wanted out." He shrugged. "Maybe he needed the money. I don't really know."

She nodded. "One thing I've learned about Uncle Rudolph. He never discussed business."

The land began to slope upward. It was hard going, and Sharon stopped to put Sophie over the saddle ahead of her. The goat fought being picked up at first, then snuggled next to Sharon and quieted down.

"That kid thinks you're her mama," Timothy commented. "We had that happen once with some baby geese. Ma bought some eggs from the neighbor lady and put them under one of our setting hens. Ma was so anxious to see them hatch out that she kept going to check on them. Next thing you know, six baby geese were following Ma everywhere she went—to the clothesline, to the outhouse, everywhere. She had to run inside the house to get away from them." He chuckled. "That's the last time she did that."

Sharon stroked Sophie's soft head.

It was close to noon when they topped a rise and drew up to let the horses blow. Before them lay rolling hills that swept toward the horizon like giant waves. A breeze covered the riders with luxurious, cooling gusts.

"I wonder why no one lives here," Sharon murmured. "It's so beautiful."

"See what I meant? One of these days I'm going to have the first house in these parts." He turned his pony north. "But this isn't the greatest. Let's keep going."

They moved ahead without speaking for another thirty minutes. Finally, the sound of a trickling stream and the cooling fingers of a soft wind over water reached them.

Ginger quickened her pace. Sophie pricked up her ears.

"Over here!" Timothy called, leading them down a small

slope to a winding stream full of rounded stones.

When they stopped, Timothy dismounted first. Then Sharon lifted Sophie, handed her down to Timothy, and slid from the saddle. Holding the goat's rope, she let her drink at the stream's edge. Ginger sank her front legs into the stream. She drank, tossed her head, and drank some more.

"Watch out!" Timothy called. "She'll end up with a bellyache."

"She's all right," Sharon replied. "She didn't get winded at all. She could have run most of the way." She knelt and wet her hands to wipe her face.

"Let's leave the horses and the kid here, and hike the rest of the way," he said. "It's not much farther."

"I don't think I could pull Ginger away from this water if I tried. She's having a marvelous time." She gazed at the swirling stream. "I'm tempted to dive in myself," she whispered, drying her face with her handkerchief.

With Timothy carrying the picnic basket, they continued their climb. Bandit raced ahead and fell back by turns, nose to the ground, tail high. Behind them, Sophie baaed loud and long.

"I hate to leave her behind," Sharon said.

He pulled in a corner of his mouth as he grinned at her. "She's got plenty of grass and water. She'll be fine for an hour or so." He laughed. "I think Sophie's not the only one who thinks you're her mama."

"*Touché*," she said.

"What?"

"That's French. It means 'you got me.'"

He was impressed. "You speak French?"

She shook her head. "I studied French. There's a big difference." She stopped to catch her breath.

"It's not much farther," he said, offering her his hand. "You can lean on me, if you want to."

She ignored his hand and forced her shaking limbs to climb. At this height, the trees thinned out and tall, spiky evergreens populated the hillside. The air was cooler, only she was sweating too much from exertion to appreciate it.

Then she stepped out of the trees and onto a wide, flat rock.

Ahead of her, Timothy watched her expression. He waited without speaking.

She turned north and gasped. The view was magnificent. Greens and browns rippled into a blue distance. The breeze was constant. It lifted her bonnet and loosened the pins in her hair. It plastered her skirts around her knees. It was glorious.

She stood there for several minutes just staring and breathing.

Timothy's delighted laugh brought her out of the trance. "You'll have to help me get this tablecloth down!" he called. "It won't stay put!"

Every time he tried to flip it out, the wind turned the red-checked square into a sail. Exasperated, Timothy stood with his boots holding down two corners while Sharon set the picnic basket on a third corner and a large stone on the fourth. He waited while she found two more stones to replace his feet.

Finally, they were able to plop down in the center.

"No problem with ants at this picnic," he said. "They'd blow clean off the edge."

She opened the picnic basket and offered it to him. "We'd better eat right out of the basket," she told him. "We'll be diving for our lunch if we don't."

Munching chicken, they sat together and enjoyed the view.

She leaned back on one hand and said, "I wish we could

stay all day, Timothy."

"Wouldn't you like to live up here?" he asked.

"The view would be great, but how would I get anything done? I'd be sitting on my front porch all day long." She reached into the basket for a biscuit.

He lay back and stared at the sky. "And what's wrong with that? Sounds like my kind of life."

"You'd get bored in a couple of days. You know you would."

He sat up. "How do you like ranch life?" he asked. "Are you going to stay here?"

"Except for the drought, I like it fine. Love it, actually."

"Oh, yeah. I forgot about Sophie."

"Don't forget Ginger," she said with a smile. "Now that I've settled in, I can't imagine living anywhere else." She watched a hawk circling at eye level before her. Wings spread, it looped and dove. Not a care in the world.

"That's me," he said, nodding at the bird. "Free as the wind."

They spent another hour, then reluctantly captured the tablecloth and headed down the mountain.

"This is the nicest day I've had in a very long time," she told him as they neared the ranch yard. "Thank you for inviting me."

He grinned. "The pleasure was all mine. We'll have to do it again."

"I can hardly wait," she said.

At that moment, a black barn cat dashed across the lane and disappeared into the corral on the right. Timothy yanked on the reins, and his pony reared. Before Sharon could fully grasp what had happened, the young man lay in a dusty heap beside Ginger.

Sharon caught a movement some distance down the fence. Just a flutter and then it was gone. Had she imagined it?

She swung down and helped Timothy to his feet. "What happened?" she asked.

Timothy stood and stared at the fence line, the corral, the barn in the distance. "Did you recognize that cat?" he asked.

"I think it's one of our barn cats," she said, puzzled. "Why?"

He grabbed his pony's reins. "I'm sorry, but I have to get home. Do you mind if I don't see you to the door?" He scrambled into the saddle and waved. "Thank you for a pleasant day!" he called, then disappeared down the trail with Bandit following close behind.

Corky's boys must have been playing ball somewhere behind the barn. She heard them shouting and laughing, but she couldn't see them in the field.

She took her time leading Ginger to the barn. Wilson was there to take the horse from her when she arrived. He avoided looking at Sharon and took Ginger directly to her stall.

Sharon openly stared at him. She'd never seen Wilson looking so pleased since she'd come to the Lazy H. But it was no use questioning him. She'd learned that much by now.

Troubled, she made her way to the house.

&

When Jason came to the house later that afternoon, she was waiting for him at the door.

"Something's going on, and I want to know what it is," she told him, stepping aside so he could enter.

"What kind of something?" he asked.

"Every time I have a guest, something embarrassing happens to him. I want to know why."

His head came up a fraction, his jaw clamped tight, and a little pink showed around his ears. "That would be hard to say, Sharon," he said slowly.

"Not hard to say. Hard to admit." She faced him square on,

a determined glint in her eyes.

His expression changed, and he stepped closer. "A girl who's had so much schooling should have all the answers, don't you think? Open your eyes, Sharon. You are a wealthy woman. What exactly do you think has been going on? Do you think those Romeos never thought about getting their hands on the Lazy H?"

He moved so close that she could see the tiny brown mole beside his mouth. His gaze burned into hers. "Which would you rather have, an opportunist who wants to use you to get what Rudolph worked so hard to build, or someone who cares for you because you're sweet, and spunky, and smart?"

When she didn't answer, he turned around and strode out the door, closing it firmly behind him.

She stared at the wood grain on the oak door. Was that all she was to Jim and Timothy? And Edward? She turned and ran to her room. It was too humiliating for words. And what about Jason? Who did he think he was, talking to her like that?

❧

Jason strode to the corral behind the barn and paused to lean his folded arms over the top rail. He told himself that he was only protecting the ranch from the greedy paws of a couple of counterfeit suitors who only wanted to pad their pockets with the rewards of Rudolph's hard work. Yet, even as he tried to rationalize his actions away, a silent voice told Jason that he was kidding himself.

❧

On Thursday, Wilson rode in from the south and came straight to the porch where Max and Sharon were shelling beans.

"I just talked to one of O'Bannon's men," he rasped. "South of our fence line, the stream is about played out."

Max asked, "Did he say what O'Bannon has in mind?"

"He said he had no idea, but it doesn't look good." Wilson took off his hat and blotted his forehead with his shirtsleeve. "I'm afraid they might cut the fence again."

Sharon swallowed to ease the growing knot in her throat. She needed advice, but from whom?

twelve

On Sunday morning, Jason had just come to take Sharon to church when Wilson came to the house. "There's about a hundred head of Double O cattle stomping through the water hole," he said.

Jason turned to Sharon. "What do you say, Boss Lady?" he asked. "What now?"

"I don't know." Her heart was thumping in her throat. "What would Uncle Rudolph do?"

Jason hesitated.

Wilson scratched his stubbled jaw. "Miss Sharon, Rudolph kept the peace because of who he was, not what he did."

"I need some time to think," she burst out. "I'm afraid this will end up in gunplay. We don't want that, do we?"

Neither of them answered. Helping Sharon aboard, Jason climbed up on the other side and shook the reins. The buckboard rumbled down the trail.

"Don't you have anything to say that would help me?" she demanded of Jason after a few minutes. "I thought you promised to take care of things for me."

"What do you want me to do?" he flung back. "Grab some rifles and run them off? If we do that, we're burning bridges that will never be mended with the Double O. Someone may be killed, maybe Corky or Wilson." He turned to her. "How would you feel about that?"

When she didn't answer he went on, "On the other hand, let's say we do nothing. We'll end up in the same shape as O'Bannon—our cattle bawling for water and maybe dying."

Jason's mother was feeling too ill to come out, and Lucy decided to stay with her. As soon as the McCormick family climbed into the back of the buckboard, they were on their way.

For the rest of the ride into town Sharon sat silent. When they reached the church, she spotted Edward Kellerman's horse tied with the rest. She met his gaze when she stepped through the door, and he came to meet her.

"What is it?" he asked. "You look like you've got something on your mind."

Without answering, she turned back through the door and kept walking until they were some distance from the closest listener. "O'Bannon's men drove some cattle onto our land. They're stomping through the water hole. As low as it is, soon it will be pure sludge." She gripped his arm. "What am I going to do? I'm afraid there will be shooting."

His face stiffened. "This is a wild country, Sharon. Sometimes you have to protect what's yours with guns. It's not easy, but it's necessary." He placed his hand over hers. "Send your hands over there and drive those cows back—the Double O cowboys, too. Do you want your own cattle to die of thirst? That's the only issue you can think about now."

From his coat pocket he drew several papers folded together. "I was going to talk to you about this later, but this is as a good a time as any." He unfolded the papers. In large curly script the heading said POWER OF ATTORNEY. He handed it to her. "I've been thinking about what you said about needing help. I'm willing to put myself on the line for you, Sharon." He smiled gently into her eyes. "Whatever you need, I'm ready to stand up for you. You know that."

She scanned the pages. "What is this?"

"It's only a formality," he said, reaching into his pocket for a pen in a narrow leather case. "Sign that and I'll be able to take care of your business without having to bother you with every little detail. I'll give you reports once a month or once a quarter. You won't have to worry about anything at all."

She glanced at the closely written document. The words were flowery and so was the handwriting. She didn't have time to read it all now. She handed it back to him. "I can't sign anything today, Edward. It's Sunday. Besides, I've got too much on my mind to think about something like that."

He hesitated, then slowly took it from her. "How about if I call on you later in the week when you'll have time to read it over?" he asked.

She nodded. "That would be best, I think." She smiled up at him. "Thank you."

He took her hand and folded it over his bent elbow. "You are quite welcome."

She walked with him to the church door, then pulled away, imagining every female eye in the building turning to watch her come in late with Edward Kellerman.

The congregation was standing and singing when they arrived. With a nod, Edward returned to his seat on the left. Sharon found a seat with the McCormick family.

If only there were a chapter and verse in the Bible to give her the answer to her dilemma. Then again, maybe there was one, but she didn't know where to find it.

The preacher droned on and on. A fly buzzed around Sharon's pew. Roddy swatted at it until his mother jostled his arm. Would the message ever end? Sharon couldn't focus on a single word.

Later that afternoon, after leaving the McCormick family at their cabin, Jason said, "I'm not staying at my mother's place this afternoon. We have to deal with the water situation before sunset."

She nodded but didn't speak. What was she going to do?

❧

Immediately after lunch, Sharon changed into riding clothes while Jason took the buckboard to the barn. When she came outside, Jason was in the saddle and leading Ginger toward the house. Wilson and Corky were mounted and waiting in the yard. When the bay mare saw Sharon, she nickered and picked up her pace. Sharon waited on the porch for an easier mount.

"Ginger! You good girl." She stroked the mare's face.

"You sure have won her over," Jason said. "No one cottoned much to Ginger before you came. She was too wild."

She sent him an arched look. "Ginger and I have a lot in common," she said and stepped into the stirrup.

The men had rifle scabbards on their horses, and they were wearing their gun belts. Sharon's hands were shaking, her heart thumping in her neck. She sent up a heartfelt prayer for safety. If only there was some way to settle this whole situation with no losers.

"Let's take it easy," Jason said as they set out. "It's too hot to get the horses lathered up."

Corky and Wilson moved ahead. Jason rode beside Sharon while she rambled on about Sophie eating the tail end of her apron string the last time she was in the pen. "One day soon, I'm going to tie a rope to her collar and take her riding with me. She had so much fun when we went to Chimney Rock."

When they all paused for a drink from their warm canteens, Jason said, "There must be some way to get through this drought without killing each other. If we think hard enough, we should be able to figure something out."

Sharon asked, "What about a well? We have a couple of them at the house. Could we drill for water out on the range and pump it for the cows?"

Corky let out a short laugh.

"It's not practical," Jason told her. "With the water table this low, we'd have a bad time drilling. Besides that, do you have any idea how much water one cow needs every day? And how much we'd have to pump? It would keep a man busy all day long."

They rode on in silence for a few minutes. There wasn't a bird, a rabbit, or even a lizard anywhere in sight. Every living creature was hiding from the glare of that broiling sun.

As they neared the water hole, a cowboy on a paint horse came into view. When he saw them, he whistled to someone out of sight.

A milling mass of about one hundred fifty cows were around and in the water hole. They were bawling as four cowboys tried to herd them south. When a handful moved away, a dozen more turned around and came back to the water.

"Whose cows are those?" Sharon asked. "All I see are Lazy H brands."

"They're all mixed up," Jason said, disgusted. "Getting them separated could be half a day's work the way things are going."

Luther Heinburg moved his mustang through the swirling herd and came near enough to shout, "We're trying to move them out!" he called. "We're not having much luck!" He took off his hat and rubbed his face with a grimy red bandanna, then urged his horse closer. The stallion fought the bit and edged around.

Finally, Heinburg was close enough for conversation. "Some mavericks busted down your fence. They must have smelled water. Once it was down, the rest of them followed." He took his hat off but still held it up to shade his eyes. "This weren't our doing, Miss Hastings," he said.

Both Wilson and Corky had their chins tucked down,

disbelieving looks on their faces. Jason's arm stretched toward his rifle butt. Sharon reached out in a quelling gesture.

Jason stared at her. She held his eyes for a moment, then turned toward Heinburg.

"We both have a problem, Mr. Heinburg," she said. "So does everyone in this section of the territory. We want to work things out so everyone wins. I hope you'll help us do that." She gazed toward the water hole. "The trouble is, once the water gets so low and too many cows come around, they'll churn it into mud and make it useless. Then we'll both lose."

Heinburg replaced his hat. "I wish there were some easy answers. I truly do. Our groundwater is getting so low that the cows can hardly drink it. That's why they moved up here." He glared at the yellow sky. "Why doesn't it rain? Half a day would turn this whole thing around."

Jason scanned the jostling, bumping herd. "Looks like only about a third of them are ours. Don't worry about culling them out. Roundup is only six weeks away. We'll separate them then."

Heinburg relaxed a little. "I wish I could tell you we'd have the beeves off your land today, but they're giving the boys a bad time."

"Wilson and Corky will help you out," Jason said. He glanced toward the men, and they set off toward the herd.

Luther Heinburg wheeled his horse around and rejoined his men.

After a few minutes, Sharon voiced the question that had been on her mind for days. "What if the water hole dries up?"

"As far I as I know, that's never happened. But if it does, we'll round them up and head for the hills," Jason said shortly. "There's water farther north. Our source is the mountains. There's always water there."

In her heart Sharon cried out to the Lord. They needed

help. Why didn't He answer? She couldn't understand it. There were so many things that she couldn't understand. Why had her parents died when she was so young? Why had she come into so much responsibility before she was ready? The trouble was, no one could really give her answers except to say, "God knows best," or "God never puts on us more than we can bear." To Sharon, those were no answers at all.

They were almost to the ranch when Sharon asked, "Jason, what is a power of attorney?"

"A what?" He moved closer to hear better.

"A document called a power of attorney. Edward Kellerman brought one to me and wanted me to sign it."

"Is that right?" His voice had a cynical edge. "I always knew there was something shady about that guy. He's trying to run a ringer on you."

Her mouth tightened. "Why do you say that? He's a nice guy—polite, refined. . ."

Jason spurred his horse ahead so she couldn't see his face.

It was a simple question. Why didn't he give her a simple answer?

Hot and weary and disgruntled, she didn't try to catch up with him. They rode into the ranch apart. Without a word, he took Ginger's reins from her and went into the barn. She didn't see him again for the rest of the day.

thirteen

The next morning over biscuits and pan gravy, Wilson drawled, "We worked on them beeves for nigh on four hours before we got them headed back to the Double O. Corky and I checked that fence, and Heinburg was telling the truth. It was knocked down this time, not cut."

Jason set his fork on his plate and leaned back in his chair to give Wilson his full attention.

The cowhand went on, "Once we broke the ice, Heinburg's men were decent hombres." He forked a bite of biscuit. "I'm glad we didn't draw down on 'em."

Jason picked up his fork. "Why don't we ride over to O'Bannon's place and have a talk with him?" he asked Sharon. "He's a fairly reasonable man. Maybe together we can come up with a compromise."

"That's a great idea," Sharon told him. "I'm ready to ride as soon as we finish here." She glanced at Max and winked. "Wrap up one of those dried apple pies you made yesterday."

❧

Two hours later, Jason and Sharon arrived at the Double O spread, a place about the size of the Lazy H. The house was a little larger than Sharon's house, with two floors instead of one, but the rest of the place was about the same: a giant barn, several corrals, and a long, low bunkhouse. Somewhere toward the back of the property, a dog was barking loud and long.

Leaving their horses a short distance from the barn, Sharon and Jason took a few steps toward the open doors when a large red-haired man stepped outside. He wore a green-and-black checked shirt with the sleeves rolled up to the elbows and the collar open. His face was set.

His voice rumbled from deep in his chest. "Riordan," he said. "I was about to come and see you." He waved his meaty hand toward a couple of backless benches. "Have a seat. It's cooler out here than inside."

Jason shook the man's hand and said, "Jared O'Bannon, meet Sharon Hastings, Rudolph's niece. She's the new owner of the Lazy H."

With a bland expression, he faced Sharon.

Sharon smiled and offered her hand. He shook it and gave her a curt nod.

When they were seated, Jared O'Bannon found a place across from them and started right in. "Miss Hastings, I owe you an apology for my men cutting your fence." He looked her in the eyes. "It won't happen again."

He let out a heavy breath and rubbed his jaw. "My groundwater is about gone. When cattle get thirsty, they'll knock down the Rock of Gibraltar to get to water. I can't promise they'll never come on your land again."

"Your apology is accepted, Mr. O'Bannon," she said. "We came here today to try to come up with a solution to both our problems." She smiled. "I don't think neighbors should act like they're in a contest, with one winning and the other losing. I hope we can get through the drought with both of us coming out on top."

"We came to see if we could help each other out," chimed Jason.

O'Bannon said, "I don't know what to tell you, son. If we don't see rain soon, we're all gonna lose our shirts."

Jason leaned back and crossed his right ankle over his left knee. "There's still water northeast of here in the foothills.

Most of it is government land. What would you think of driving our herds up thataway?"

O'Bannon shook his head. "I've got a bumper crop of new calves this year. They can travel a little ways, but you're talking twenty or thirty miles." He leaned back against a porch post, considering. "Of course, if the drought goes on we'll lose them anyway, and their mothers, too."

Sharon said, "The water hole is so low that it can't last much longer with the cattle milling around in it."

"I've got my hands watching that section of the fence to keep them from busting through," O'Bannon said. "But that's not to say some canny renegade won't find a place down the line to cross over."

"Maybe it'll rain before we have to do anything," Sharon said, standing. "We're praying that way."

As he stood, O'Bannon muttered, "I'm thinking of selling out and moving to Durango. This water problem is making an old man out of me, and it's killing my wife."

Sharon said, "Would Mrs. O'Bannon mind if I stopped at the house for a few minutes? I'd very much like to meet her."

He nodded. "She'd like that. Go on around the house. She's washing clothes in the backyard." He turned to Jason. "I've got a sick mare. Would you mind taking a look at her?"

The men moved into the barn, and Sharon strode to Ginger to fetch the box tied behind the saddle. A few minutes later, she rounded the house and saw a tall, slim woman bent over a washboard. She wore no sunbonnet, and her face showed the effects of countless hours in the sun. Her hair was completely gray.

At Sharon's call, she straightened and rubbed suds from her arms. She waved, then moved to a pump nearby and worked the handle.

"Hello," Sharon said when she drew nearer. "I'm Sharon

Hastings from the Lazy H."

Rinsing her arms, Mrs. O'Bannon nodded. "It's kind of you to stop by," she said wearily. "Would you like a drink while I've got the water running?" At Sharon's nod, she lifted the tin ladle hanging by the side of the pump and filled it.

Sharon handed her the pie and took the ladle. The water was cool. It must have come from far down.

"I'm Peggy," the older woman said. She opened the box lid. "Well, what do you know?" she said, brightening. "Jared is partial to apple pie. It's very kind of you to bring it."

They exchanged small talk for a few minutes, then Sharon excused herself and headed for the barn. What a depressing life, she thought. The Lazy H had a family atmosphere, a team spirit. Peggy was all alone, working from morning to night. How did she stand it?

When Sharon and Jason were on their way, she flexed her shoulders and looked straight up in a gesture of relief. "That went better than I'd hoped," she said.

Jason grinned at her. "I believe you won him over."

She told him about meeting Peggy O'Bannon. "What a depressing life! And she's a nice person, Jason, a really nice person. When I think that once she was young with hopes and dreams like Lucy and I. . ."

She rambled on for a few minutes, then sighed. "Ranching seems like such a hard way to make a living."

His expression grew serious. "You are right," he said. "It seems like there's always something—too much rain, not enough rain, hoof-and-mouth scares, low beef prices, or something else that no one ever heard of yet."

"Why do people stay here for years and years?"

His eyes scanned the horizon. "There's your answer. It's the life—open sky, room to ride, nobody breathing down your neck. Can you imagine Corky or Wilson wearing a white shirt with sleeve garters and saying, 'Would you like anything else, miss?' while they filled a grocery sack?" He chuckled. "Or Max slinging hash in a restaurant with people barking orders at him from morning 'til night?"

She shook her head. "Not in a million years."

"They'd make about the same amount of money, or maybe even more. But would they want to?" He paused to look at her. "Would I?"

At that moment, a rifle report echoed across the range. Sharon looked around to see where it came from. She felt a sudden burning in her left side and looked down. A deep red spot grew to the size of a quarter, then a silver dollar. She tried to touch it, but her arm wouldn't come up.

She tried to call Jason. Then the edges of her vision turned dark. . . .

fourteen

Jason heard the rifle report and saw the shock on Sharon's face. He didn't fully understand what had happened until he saw her slump and begin to slide from the saddle. Wheeling his horse nearer, he caught her as she collapsed.

He swung his leg in front of him over the saddle, grabbed her shoulders, and slipped to the ground. He lay her down as gently as he could to see where she was hurt. A spreading bloodstain on her left side told the story. There was a hole in her shirt, and he used that to tear an opening wide enough for him to stuff his handkerchief against the bullet wound.

Scanning the horizon, he tried to see who had fired that shot. Stark horror replaced the panic of the moment. Who would do such a fiendish thing? Was he still out there, waiting for a clearer target?

Jason had to get Sharon to safety. Whistling for his horse, he forced the animal to lie down until he could get Sharon across the saddle. After the horse stood up, Jason mounted, put his arms around her, and held her against him.

Traveling as fast as he could in that awkward position, he made a beeline for his mother's cabin and prayed that Sharon would live until he got there. Ginger whinnied and galloped after them.

The thing that scared him most was the growing slick spot on her dress. It spread across her middle and down her skirt. Her head bent back to rest against his shoulder, and she never stirred once.

Bellowing for help the moment he rode into the yard, he

waited only seconds until Lucy ran outside.

When she saw Sharon, she drew up and her hands flew to her mouth. "What happened?" she squealed.

"Someone shot her," he rasped. "I didn't see who it was. Help me get her inside. I've got to get the doctor."

He eased Sharon's limp form down and Lucy lowered her to the ground. He lunged from the saddle to carry Sharon into the house. Blood had soaked the entire front of her dress. Her face had a greenish tinge, and her lips were white.

"Take her to my room!" Lucy called after him.

His mother was in the rocking chair when he stepped inside. She gasped when she saw him but didn't say a word.

Lucy dashed around him to open the door to the back bedroom. She tore back the covers, so Jason could lay Sharon on the sheet. Not stopping in to even wash his hands, he dashed past Lucy toward the front door. Outside, he grabbed Ginger's reins and leaped into the saddle.

❧

Lucy ran for a basin of hot water, scissors, and a roll of bandages. As she moved, she called out to her mother what Jason had told her.

With her head against the back of the rocking chair, Mrs. Riordan gazed at the ceiling and called aloud, "Lord Jesus, keep Thy hand upon our girl. Give wings to Jason's horse. . . ." While Lucy worked over Sharon, Mrs. Riordan never stopped praying.

Lucy used the small tear Jason had made to finish tearing the dress off of the injured girl. She pressed a small pad against the wound until the bleeding was only an ooze. Cleansing around the wound, she applied a bandage and arranged one of her old nightgowns over Sharon's form. Then she covered Sharon with a faded quilt. In spite of the heat of the day, her skin felt cold to the touch.

After that, all Lucy could do was sit beside the bed and join in her mother's prayers.

❧

The doctor was at his apartment over his office when Jason arrived. "Sharon's hurt!" he shouted as the doctor opened the door. "Someone shot her! You have to come right away!"

Dr. Lanchester hurried into his office, pulled open a drawer, and picked up several items to drop into his black Gladstone bag. The next minute he was following Jason outside.

"Let me ride your horse back," the doctor said. "Saddle my horse and bring him out."

Jason veered toward the stable and soon heard Ginger's pounding hoofbeats fading down the street. He paused to wash off his hands under the faucet near the stable.

Saddling the doctor's horse was no small matter with his hands trembling. His arms felt weak and he couldn't concentrate. The horse sensed Jason's distress and pranced around the stall. Finally, Jason stepped away. He leaned against the rail and closed his eyes for a full minute, then grabbed the cinch strap again.

Fifteen minutes later, Jason was in the saddle. As the ground moved under him, his mind was racing. Who would want Sharon dead? It made no sense. He was beginning to wonder if life ever made sense the way things had been going these past three months.

He kept the horse to a gallop until the cabin came into view.

Lucy threw herself into Jason's arms when he stepped inside. She was crying.

Holding his sister, Jason's breath stopped for moment. What had happened?

His mother said, "The doctor is taking out the bullet. He says it's only a flesh wound, but she's lost too much blood.

She may not be able to stand the surgery."

Lucy lifted her apron and dried her eyes. "Who did this to her?" she demanded.

"It was a rifle shot from inside a stand of trees. I couldn't see anyone, and I was more worried about taking Sharon to safety than chasing the guy." He tore off his Stetson and raked his fingers through his hair.

"How could someone do this? Whoever he is, he won't be safe in the territory once he's caught." He flexed his fingers. "He won't be safe in the whole country as long as I'm alive."

For the next thirty minutes, they talked about possibilities and suspects but got nowhere. Jason paced in front of the fireplace, tearing at his hair and scowling.

Finally the doctor came out.

Jason lunged at him. "How is she?"

"She survived the surgery," he said, worried, "but she's terribly weak. I'm concerned that she hasn't regained consciousness. I poured whiskey into the wound to sterilize it, and she didn't react at all." He turned to Lucy and gave her a paper envelope. "Give her this when she wakes up. I wrote the dosages on it." He pulled out his pocket watch. "It's twenty past five. I'll be back in three hours."

Jason shook his hand. "Thanks, Doc."

"If you need me, come a-running" was his only good-bye.

Jason turned toward the bedroom door. "Lucy, check to be sure she's decent. I've got to see her."

With a questioning glance at her brother's intense expression, Lucy eased the door open and peered inside, then opened the door wider. Sharon lay with her head on the pillow, a quilt tucked up under her chin. Her French twist had fallen down, but the pins were still in her hair, popping up at odd angles. Wispy strands of blond hair clung to her face.

When Lucy stepped aside, Jason crept into the room. He

felt a physical pain in his chest at seeing Sharon so still and white. What would he do without her? How could he go on?

He dropped to his knees beside the bed and gently clasped her hand. Why did they shoot her and not him? If only he had been the target. He held her hand to his lips and prayed like he hadn't prayed in years.

Finally, Lucy pressed her hand against his shoulder. "Better let her rest," she whispered.

Slowly, reluctantly, he stood and gently replaced Sharon's hand on the quilt. Three steps and he was back in the living room.

Lucy stared at his shirt. "We'll have to throw that out," she said. "There's no way I'll ever get it clean."

He glanced down and realized for the first time that his shirt was covered with blood.

Lucy gave him a hard look. "You've got it bad, haven't you, brother?"

He blinked at her as though looking through a dense fog. "What are you talking about?"

She unbuttoned his shirt and pulled it off of him while he stared at her.

Lucy leaned forward to whisper, "You're in love with her, you idiot. It's written all over you in giant letters."

Jason shook his head to clear it. He had to sit down somewhere. "Lucy," he said, "what am I going to do?"

She stepped away from him. "You're going to scrub from head to toe while I fetch you clean clothes. Then you're going to pray." Her voice faltered. Suddenly, she put her arms around him and squeezed hard. "What if she dies, Jason? How could we bear it?"

They clung to each other while Lucy cried. Their mother's voice, reedy and quavering, filled the room. " 'Oh, God, our help in ages past, our hope for years to come. . . .' "

Her children came to her, knelt beside her chair, and sang with her to the end of the verse.

With her hands on their shoulders, she prayed as though God were standing right there in the room with them. And He was.

Around seven that evening, Corky knocked at the cabin door. Jason answered and stepped outside to talk to him.

"Max has been worried sick because Sharon didn't come back to the house," Corky said. "I saw Ginger in your corral and wondered what had happened."

Jason thumped his fist against the porch post. "On the way back from O'Bannon's place somebody shot Sharon. It's a flesh wound in her side. The doc says she's lost too much blood. She may not pull through."

Corky sucked air between his teeth. "Where did it happen?"

Jason told him where they had been riding when it happened. "It seemed to come from the northeast," he finished. "Maybe from that big grove of desert willow."

Corky nodded. "Wilson and I will head out that way at first light. Maybe we can spot something, some sign of who was there."

"Look after things, will you, Corky? I'll stay here until I know something more about her condition."

Corky moved to his horse tied nearby. "I'll let the men know what's happened." He swung to the saddle and set out at a trot.

Jason stayed on the porch for a while. His feelings ran so deep that he couldn't express them. He could only cry out, "Please, help us!"

❧

The first thing Sharon knew was a burning pain deep in her side. She tried to move to ease it and got a stab from the effort. She moaned and tried to open her eyes.

Cool fingers touched her forehead. "Sharon, you're okay. You are with me, and you're going to be all right." It was Jason. What was he doing in her room? Again blackness closed over her.

Sometime later, she swung back the cover. Too hot.

When she managed to open her eyes, Lucy was bending over her, wiping her face with a cool cloth.

"What happened?" Sharon mumbled. She felt so tired she could hardly breathe.

"You had an accident on the way back from the Double O ranch. The doctor had to stitch your side. That's why you're in pain." She helped Sharon sit up enough to drink from a glass.

When she lay back, Sharon murmured, "Jason."

"He's outside. He's been here for two days, waiting for you wake up." She gave Sharon a gentle smile and hurried out.

The next moment, Jason rushed to her side. He didn't say anything, but the look on his face reached her deep inside. She tried to tell him, but she was too weak. A single tear slid down toward her ear.

He touched her face and wiped it away. "You're safe now. You're with me and you're going to be all right."

She nestled her cheek against his hand and closed her eyes.

≈

Jason cradled Sharon's cheek until a cramp forced him to move his hand away. She hadn't cried until he came in. He wanted to fold her into his arms and never let go.

"It's ten o'clock," Lucy whispered from behind him. "You ought to get some rest. You've had a long day."

He nodded and stood. "I'll sleep a couple of hours, then come downstairs so you can sleep." He gazed down at Sharon's sleeping form. He hadn't been able to leave the house. Corky and Wilson had taken over Jason's chores for a few days. There was no way he could think of anything besides Sharon.

Lucy touched his arm and he came to himself. "There's some corn bread and buttermilk in the kitchen, if you need to eat," she whispered, then pressed him toward the door.

Eat? Would he ever eat again? He stumbled up the stairs and flung himself on the cot he'd slept in since he was a boy, and instantly fell into an exhausted sleep.

෨

When the doctor arrived on the third day, Sharon was awake. He completed his examination and invited Jason and Lucy into the room. "She's going to be fine," he said, beaming at the patient. "You gave us a bad scare, young lady," he said. "I prescribe two weeks of complete rest before you can go home. Drink as much water as you can hold, and don't make any sudden moves."

He shook Jason's hand on his way out and grinned at Lucy.

When the door closed behind him, his mother said, "God be praised. Lucy, come and help me up, so I can see our girl."

With Lucy holding tightly around her middle, she tottered in and took the only chair in the room. "Child," she said, "God has His hand on you. He's spared your life twice now. You are blessed."

Sharon's eyes filled with tears. She couldn't speak.

With a pat on Sharon's hand, Mother stood and slowly made her way out. "You kids stop hovering over her now. Let her rest, or she'll never get better."

Jason waited until his mother crossed the threshold before he came into the room. "I won't stay long," he said. He pulled the chair closer and sat, bending close to Sharon's face.

She said, "Max?"

"He's coming over tomorrow when you're stronger. He was mighty worried about you—we all were." He smiled into her eyes and she felt warm and safe.

That warm, safe feeling lasted for the rest of the time she

stayed at the Riordan cabin. After the first week, Jason left at times to attend to ranch business, but he continued to sleep there. When she was strong enough, they'd sit on the porch in the evenings, listening to the cricket chorus, slowly rocking and talking until Lucy came to shoo Sharon to bed.

"Do you have any idea who did this to me?" she asked him on the eighth day.

His face grew grim. "I wish I could say we knew who it was, but I never got a look at him. All we know is that someone used a rifle with a scope. Otherwise, I'd have seen him." He stopped rocking and stretched out his legs. "Wilson couldn't spot any sign. He didn't halfway know where to look."

She shivered. "What if he's still out there? What if he comes back to try again?" She hugged herself and scanned the darkness.

"No one could see us sitting here. The light from the window is too dim."

"But what about later? Will I be able to ride Ginger again? Will I have to stay like a prisoner in the house?"

He came out of his seat and squatted beside her. He gazed into her eyes. "I'm going to take care of you, Sharon. I'll find out who did this if it's the last thing I ever do. I promise you."

Sharon forgot the danger. She forgot the crickets and the ache in her side.

He drew closer.

She tilted her face toward his.

"Sharon?" Lucy called as she opened the door. "It's eight o'clock, time for you to go to bed."

Quickly, Jason stood and stepped away. "I'll help her inside," he told his sister.

Lucy went inside but didn't close the door.

Jason offered Sharon his arm and braced her with his hand, so she could stand. Any full-body movements still gave her pain. She grunted as she came to her feet.

They moved slowly through the living room and into Sharon's temporary room. She curled her fingers around his arm, and he covered her hand with his.

"Can I get you some water?" he asked when she eased herself down to the edge of the bed. When she nodded, he poured her a glass from a metal pitcher close to the bed. She drank it, handed him the glass, and lay back.

Jason closed the door and left her in the darkness.

Sharon let her body meld into the feather tick under her. Her eyes were closed, but she could see Jason clearly. She could feel his nearness and the warmth of his gaze. If only she didn't have to go back to the ranch. If only she could stay here like this, safe and cared for—with Jason—forever.

fifteen

Sharon's recovery was steady and without any infection. On the morning of the sixteenth day, she hugged Lucy and said good-bye. "There's no way I could ever thank you for all you've done for me," she said.

"I'm going to miss you," Lucy replied. "I should be thanking you for the company." She gave Sharon's hand a squeeze. "I'll come and see you before long."

Sharon said, "Tell Mother I said good-bye. I didn't want to wake her. She gets precious little sleep."

Jason set a box under the iron step on the surrey and helped her up. She gripped the edge of the seat as the surrey began to sway. With many anxious glances in her direction, Jason kept the horse to a slow pace. The journey seemed endless.

When they reached the ranch house, Jason lifted her off her feet and gently set her down. He held her for moment as she got her balance. Then Max burst out the door, and Jason turned her loose.

"I'd hoped you wouldn't come until after lunch," Max burst out. "I didn't want you to see the house like this. Someone broke in last night. Everything's a mess. I think they were looking for something."

Sharon's already pale face turned ashen when she saw the floor strewn with torn ledgers, broken tally books, and loose papers. The sofa cushions were ripped open, and the rocking chairs lay on their sides. Desk drawers lay upside down with their contents thrown across the floor.

Her steps faltered. Max came to support her other side, and they got her onto her bed in short order. In her room, her dresses lay in a heap on the floor, her toiletries dumped all over the dresser top.

"I want to change," she said weakly. "I had a gown in there." She pointed toward the overturned trunk at the end of her bed. "If you will find it for me, I can do the rest."

&

Jason found the clothing and laid it on the bed. When he closed the door, she was pushing herself to a standing position beside the bed.

"Max," Jason said, "did you hear anything last night?"

The little man's face was troubled. "The horses were restless, but that was all. We figured there was a coyote in the neighborhood."

"There was a coyote in the neighborhood, all right. He was in here." He scanned the room, disgusted. "All this is going to upset her to no end. We've got to get it cleaned up right away. I'd ask Lucy, but she's had all she can take with two invalids to care for these past two weeks." He bent over to gather papers into a stack.

Max started picking things up around the desk. "Whoever it was, he had to be looking for something," he repeated. "There's nothing in here worth stealing."

They worked for a good half hour and finally had the floor cleared, but the desk was still in shambles. Jason closed the lid on a jumbled mess. Sharon would have to sort things out when she felt better. As the owner, she was the only one who could decide what was important enough to keep.

Leaving Max to his kitchen work, Jason went out to the barn and didn't return until the triangle jangled for lunch. When he came in, Max had a tray made up for Sharon. Jason took it from him and carried it to her room. He knocked briefly, then entered when she called out.

Sitting up on the bed, she had a robe tied around her. She frowned at the food. Her stomach felt like lead. "I don't think I can eat anything."

"Max made chicken soup with egg noodles. Eat two small bites to make him happy. Can you do that?" He held up a dish towel. "He sent you this so you wouldn't spill on yourself."

She tried to smile. "I should have one of those even when I'm at the table." She finished half the bowl, then handed it to him. "Are you going to eat?" she asked.

He handed her a tall glass of water. "I can eat anytime." He stared at the pile on the floor. "Will it tire you too much if I straighten up in here?"

"Quite the opposite," she said wearily. "I've been scolding myself for being such a sissy. I should be picking things up instead of lying here."

"That's just what I *don't* want you to do: scold yourself or pick anything up. That's what I'm here for."

She wrinkled her nose. "It's not proper for you to be handling my things," she said.

"Who is going to know? Just Max. And he's not skittish." He set about hanging up her dresses and stuffed the rest into the trunk and the dresser. Closing the last drawer, he said, "That wasn't so bad, was it?" He touched her foot through the quilt. "I'm going out so you can get some rest."

He disappeared through the door. Pulling off her robe, Sharon lay down and closed her eyes. She wanted to cry, but she didn't have the strength. That ride home really took it out of her.

That night Max finished tidying up the kitchen shortly after supper, then left the house. Alone in her room, Sharon lay with her eyes wide open, hearing every creak in the house and every rustling limb outside her window.

What if that man came back? He was here last night. Did he find what he was looking for? Was he watching the house, knowing that she was home?

What if he came into the house? She was too weak to even scream. The triangle was outside. What would she do?

It was well past dark when the front door groaned as it opened. Footsteps sounded like gunshots on the plank flooring. A gentle tap at her door. "Sharon?" Max said. "Are you awake?"

Pulling the quilt to her chin, Sharon said, "Max! Come in." Her breathing was quick and shallow. "You scared the life out of me."

"Honey, I'm so sorry. I should have called out when I opened the door. I came to see if you are okay."

"Would you mind sleeping in the house for a few days? What if someone came back in the middle of the night? I would be trapped in here with no way to call for help."

He put his hand on the edge of the door. "I'd be glad to do that. I'll get my things from the bunkhouse." He glanced at her empty glass on the night table. "Let me refill that while I'm here." He took the glass and disappeared.

Her eyes drifted closed, and she never knew when he brought it back.

For the next two days, Sharon felt fussed over until she was thoroughly tired of it. On the third morning, she insisted on dressing and coming out to breakfast.

"So tell me what's been happening," she said as she spread butter on a pancake. "It hasn't rained yet. I know that. What about the water hole?" She glanced at Jason and waited for his answer.

He made a show of finishing his coffee and slowly set down the cup. "Last week the water hole sank to eight inches deep. O'Bannon is out of water. His cows have smashed our fence line for over two hundred yards. There's no chance of driving them back now. They're too crazy with thirst."

Wilson added, "I rode over there yesterday. We've less than six inches now. Soon it will be totally mud."

Sharon took in the news for a moment. "Since I've had so much time to think, I was wondering if we could do this: How about if we rounded up our herd and pushed them into the foothills? At least our cows would have access to good water. We can give O'Bannon free range on our place so his cows can get to the streams to the north and east."

"There is still water in the streams up toward the north end," Wilson said. "Much of our herd is already there."

Jason nodded. "That could work, if we get started right away before they get so weak that we can't drive them." He pushed back from the table. "We really need a few extra hands."

Corky said, "Roddy and Mike can help us out. I think we'd best leave Ian to tend to the stock here."

Jason nodded. "It'll be tough going, but once we get them to the fresh water we won't have to worry about them drifting back. We can make two or three sweeps and get most of them." He glanced at Max. "Can you pack us some grub? We'll camp on the range at least one night."

Before he finished speaking, heavy footsteps sounded on the front porch. Max hurried to open the door and Jared O'Bannon stepped inside. His face was haggard, and he hadn't shaved in at least a week.

When he saw Sharon, he removed his hat. "Miss Hastings, I need to speak to you. I'm sorry, but it can't wait."

"Mr. O'Bannon," she said, "please have a seat here at the table. Would you like some hotcakes and coffee?"

He took a step toward the table. Max hurried to the kitchen. He came back with a mug of steaming black brew and set it before O'Bannon with an empty enamel plate and a clean fork.

"I'm much obliged," the big man said. His shoulders slumped against the back of the chair. "You said you wanted to find a solution to our problem," he said. "I came to see what we could work out." He licked his dry lips and raised his coffee cup.

Sharon said, "We were discussing that. Jason?"

"Sharon had an idea that may work. How about if we play leapfrog? We'll drive our cows north, up beyond our boundary into the government land in the foothills. You drive your cows into the northeast section of the Lazy H. That way, your calves won't have to travel so far. Our calves can make it into the foothills with no problem." Jason leaned back, waiting for O'Bannon's response.

The rancher sat unmoving for a long moment. He slowly turned to Sharon. "You would do that?"

"It's the best idea we could come up with. But it's not a permanent solution. If it doesn't rain for another two weeks, our water will be gone, too."

"That's true," he said, "but that would give my calves time to rest between moves."

Another knock sounded at the door and Max exclaimed, "Who else?" He hurried to the door and the next moment Edward Kellerman stepped inside. He was wearing his black suit and carrying his black leather case. He had his hat in his hand and flipped it onto a peg as he walked in.

When he saw Jared O'Bannon, Kellerman's expression darkened. "Good morning, Sharon," he said. "I see you have company."

Sharon smiled, trying to ease the atmosphere. "Have you met Jared O'Bannon, Edward?"

"Only by reputation," he said shortly.

"Sit down and have some coffee," Sharon invited. "Have you had breakfast?"

Max got Kellerman a plate and a mug of coffee, then returned to his seat.

Jason stood. "We can work out the details," he told Sharon. To O'Bannon he said, "I'll walk with you to your horse." Wilson and Corky stood with them and the ranch hands left the house.

Max started stacking plates.

Edward picked up his dishes and moved closer to Sharon. "I hope that wasn't trouble," he said as Max began rattling dishes in the dishpan.

"Not at all," Sharon said. "I think we're going to get things worked out." She glanced at his leather case lying on the table. "What brings you here so early?"

He forked two hotcakes on to his plate. "Well, first of all I wanted to see how you are. I heard you had an accident." He poured syrup.

"As you can see, I'm doing fine. I'm a little tired, but otherwise I'm as good as new."

Between bites he said, "What's O'Bannon up to? Is he pushing you to share your water? If he is, you should send your hands to the fence line with rifles. You've got to protect your rights, Sharon. Once these men see you as weak, they'll take advantage of you. That's one reason that I came out here this morning." Pushing his empty plate aside, he opened the leather case and drew out the forms he had shown her outside the church, the power of attorney. He didn't hand them to her but set them on the table.

Sharon stood up. She didn't want to discuss business. She moved into the living room, intending to sit in the rocking chair.

Edward stepped in front of her, close enough for her to notice the perfect knot in his tie. He clasped her hands in both of his and pulled them toward his lips. "You don't know how worried I was when I heard what had happened to you.

I found out only yesterday." He had a hurt expression. "I wish you had sent word. I would have been here every day."

"Edward. . ."

At that moment Jason burst through the door. He drew up, and his cheeks took on a reddish hue.

Sharon pulled her hands away. "Yes, Jason, what is it?"

He hesitated. "We're getting ready to ride. I came to fetch the grub."

"I've got it ready!" Max called from the kitchen.

Jason made a wide circle around Sharon and met Max halfway. Taking the lumpy bundle, he headed out the door without saying good-bye.

Disgruntled, Sharon sank into the rocking chair. Edward Kellerman was becoming a distinct nuisance.

Sitting on the very edge of the sofa, he reached toward her. Their knees almost met as he handed her the power of attorney papers. "If you'd like time to read this, I can take a walk for a few minutes. I hope you can understand how important this is for your protection."

She frowned. "Don't you know that I'm in the middle of a crisis? Why do you keep bothering me with this paperwork?"

He took the papers back. "I apologize. I guess I'm so worried about you that I'm not thinking straight." He folded the papers back into his case. Raising his perfectly manicured hand, he smoothed his right eyebrow. "I'm your attorney. That means I'm your friend and advisor. All this trouble is taking its toll on you, Sharon. There's no reason to put yourself in this kind of distress. I'm here to help you. I *want* to help you. But you have to let me."

He reached into his jacket and pulled a second set of papers from the inside pocket. "You'll be glad to know that your uncle's will has been recorded. And I have here an offer to buy the ranch for five thousand dollars. You might be wise to consider it."

She took the pages and read them. This was less than Rudolph had paid fifteen years before.

She shook her head and handed them back. "I can't do it."

"I think this party may double the money," he said.

She stared at him. "Why would anyone pay that much? We are having the worst drought in years."

He pursed his lips. "They probably have good reason. Cattle isn't the only thing this land could be used for."

Max stepped in from the kitchen. "I don't mean to butt in," he said, "but are you talking about the Cattlemen's Treasure?" He grinned. "You may as well be talking about gold at the end of a rainbow." He returned to the kitchen, chuckling.

Kellerman wasn't smiling.

When Sharon tried to hand the offer to him, he gently pushed it back. "You keep that," he said. "Sleep on it. You may think better of it in the morning."

She shook her head and pressed the offer toward him. "Maybe for ten thousand," she said. "But never for five thousand." She stood. "I'm awfully tired. This has been a long morning, and I need to rest now." She turned toward her room, then remembered her manners and paused to say, "Thank you for coming out, Edward."

Stuffing the papers into his pocket, he stood. "I'll check on you in a couple of days." He took his leather case, lifted his hat from its peg, and went out.

❧

When Sharon woke up from her nap, Max was frying bacon in the kitchen. He poured her a cup of coffee without her even asking and set it on the table at her place. Pouring himself a cup, he pulled the skillet to the cold side of the stove and came to join her.

"Feeling better?" he asked.

She nodded. "I can feel my strength growing every day.

Before long, I'll forget all about this weakness." She sipped her coffee.

Max rotated his cup by the handle. "I hope you don't think my nose is too long, but something about that lawyer doesn't sit right with me."

Sharon didn't reply for a moment. What was it about Edward that had irritated her this morning? "I don't exactly know what it is," she said, "but there's something wrong about him. I didn't feel it until this morning. Here I am, wounded by some unknown attacker, and all he can do is shove papers in my face." She turned toward Max with anxious eyes. "What should I do? There's no other lawyer in Farmington, is there?"

"You're right about that. But do you need one here? You could travel to Bloomfield to take care of your business if you had to."

"I'll talk to Jason about it when I get a chance."

"If all goes well, he'll be back tomorrow night." He stood and slid the skillet back into place. "I'm going to ride out to meet the hands later this afternoon with more grub. Do you feel up to pinching off some biscuits? I'll mix up the dough so you won't have to strain yourself with stirring."

"I'd be glad for something to do. Sitting still gives me cabin fever. It's bad enough in the winter but unbearable in the summer."

Max grabbed a bowl and dumped in flour, lard, and other ingredients. "Sophie's been going crazy in the nanny pen. She'll be all mighty glad to see you."

Sharon smiled softly. "I wish I could go out to see her, but I'd better wait a couple more days. She's so lively, she'll knock me down. I can't brace myself right now."

She dropped a soft lump of dough into a pan. "She may forget me by the time I'm well enough to go out."

Max snorted. "Not a chance of that. You've branded yourself all over this place, my dear, and not only in Sophie's mind."

sixteen

For nearly forty-eight hours Jason had brooded over catching Sharon and Kellerman with their heads together when he came upon them in the living room. But when Jason returned home the next afternoon, the last thing on his mind was Edward Kellerman.

Sharon was reading in the rocking chair and looked up, startled, when he burst in, his face flushed, his eyes wild. "Jason, what is it?" she cried.

Max trotted into the room to hear the news.

"We found Rudolph," Jason gasped. "Corky was riding a ridgeline about ten miles north of here and spotted Rudolph's red plaid shirt at the bottom of a gully. I've come to fetch the buckboard to bring him home. I'm going to take a door loose from the tack room to put the body on and hoist it up."

"Take an old quilt to wrap him in!" Max called over his shoulder as he hustled toward the spare room. He returned with the blanket in his arms. Jason grabbed it and rushed out.

Max sidled up to the sofa and sank down. "Now don't this beat all," he murmured. "How in the world did Rudolph get to be ten miles up in the foothills? He would have never ridden off our range without telling someone first."

"Somebody took a shot at *me*," Sharon said. "Who's to say they didn't shoot him first? If Jason hadn't been with me, who knows? You may have never found me, either."

Max rubbed his head. "I can't understand why anyone would do such a thing. Rudolph was a decent man. He always went the extra mile to help someone in trouble. He didn't care if a man had been in prison, he'd still help him."

"Well, someone had it in for him," Sharon said. "We need to figure out who. Mixed in there somewhere is a great big *why* running underground like a subterranean river." Her brows drew together. "Maybe we've been looking at it wrong. Instead of looking for enemies, maybe we should start thinking about people who should love Uncle Rudolph." Her eyes widened. "Maybe they *should* love him, but they resent him instead."

"You may have something there, missy," he said, getting to his feet and setting off toward the kitchen. "Let me study on that while I finish supper."

Several hours later, the men brought the body home and put it in the tack room. They couldn't bring it into the house because of the smell.

Soon after, the sheriff arrived on horseback, and the undertaker in a closed wagon. Put together, the two men had lived more than a hundred years in these parts. Their set faces showed that very little surprised them anymore.

After they examined Rudolph's body, Sheriff Quentin Feingold met with Sharon and the hands outside the barn. More than six feet tall, he was wide and thick from his neck to his belt buckle. "From what we can tell," he said in a deep, gravelly voice, "Rudolph was shot twice through the chest and then dumped into that ravine. He must have died almost instantly." He paused, then engulfed Sharon's hand in his. "My condolences, Miss Hastings," he said. "This is bad business."

"Thank you, Sheriff," she said. "We'll come into town tomorrow morning to make the arrangements."

"There's no hurry," he told her. "The doc will have to make a complete examination before we can let you bury him. But you can go ahead and see Darien," he said, jerking his neck toward the undertaker, Darien Michaels, who was busy at his wagon, "and the parson anytime you wish, to let them know your plans."

He turned to Jason. "Son, I'll need to meet with you and your men to get your statements about what happened the day Rudolph disappeared."

Jason nodded. "We'll come into town and get that taken care of."

The officials loaded the remains in the undertaker's wagon and left together, anxious to get back to town before dark.

As the hands ambled back into the barn, Jason walked with Sharon to the house.

"How horrible," Sharon said. "I can't imagine that someone we know did this to Uncle Rudolph." Suddenly, she sounded hopeful. "Maybe it was one of the Double O hands, or some stranger passing through."

"It would be nice to think it's someone without a face or a personality, someone who's like a paper doll cutout to us," Jason said, "but that's not likely, Sharon."

She told him about her conversation with Max that afternoon. "What if the gunman wasn't someone who hated Uncle Rudolph? What if it was someone that he had helped? Someone who should love him?"

They climbed the porch steps and sat together on the short bench to the right of the door.

Sharon went on, "Do you know who Uncle Rudolph has helped recently?"

Jason scanned her eager face. "Are you wearing yourself out with all this?" he asked with a worried note in his voice. "You mustn't get too worked up."

She grew impatient. "I'm trying to tell you something important."

"So am I," he replied, still gazing at her.

Meeting his eyes, Sharon's tone softened to almost a whisper.

"I'm getting stronger every day."

He leaned closer.

With loud, clomping boots, Max stepped up and scraped a bench across the porch so he could sit across from them.

Jason said, "Max, we were about to list off the people Rudolph has helped. We're wondering if any of them may be his murderer."

Max nodded. "Sharon and I were talking about that earlier."

"Let's see. . ." Jason extended one finger at every name. "There's the Widow Braddock who ended up selling her place and moving to Santa Fe. Zach Ingles who owns the general store and is about the richest man in town, Rev. Nelson, Corky. . .and Sharon."

She gasped. "Me?"

He bent his little finger back toward his palm. "Just joshing you," he said, grinning. "As a matter of fact, I should put one finger up for me and Ma and Lucy. He sure did help us when Pa died." He stretched out his little finger again.

"Put up another finger for me," Max said. "He helped me out, and not only once, neither."

With that, Jason let his hand rest on his leg. "Looks like we're barking up the wrong tree," he told Sharon. "I can't imagine anyone on that list wanting to hurt Rudolph. It's got to be someone else."

"The Cattleman's Treasure," Max blurted out. "That's got to be it."

"That old saw?" Jason retorted. "That's pure hogwash. There is no treasure."

Max said, "We know that, but you know how rumors grow in small towns. There may be some folks who believe it."

"Even if the rumor were true," Sharon said, "why shoot Uncle Rudolph?"

Max held up his pudgy hand. "Because he wouldn't sell at

any price. Maybe someone wanted to buy the ranch and they figured it'd be easier to buy his estate than convince him to sell."

"They didn't figure on him having an heir," Jason added. "That would answer for why they took a shot at Sharon, too."

She froze. "Edward just brought me an offer to buy the ranch. It was all drawn up and legal."

"Do you still have it?" Jason asked.

She shook her head. "I wouldn't take it from him."

"Too bad," Max said. "We could have checked to see who wanted to buy it."

"I read it," Sharon said. "It wasn't a person. It was a company." She leaned her head back and closed her eyes. "What was it? It was a funny name."

"How much did they offer?" Jason asked.

"Five thousand dollars, and he said the party would be willing to double it."

Jason whistled. "That's a lot of money for a ranch in the middle of the worst drought in years."

"He said. . ." Sharon hesitated, trying to remember the exact words. "'Cattle isn't the only thing this land could be used for.'"

Max nodded. "That's when I came into the living room and told him that if he meant the Cattleman's Treasure, there was no such thing."

"I don't want to hurt you," Jason told Sharon, "but I'm afraid your friend Edward Kellerman has got something deep going on under all his pretty ways."

Max added, "It don't look good, and that's a fact."

Sharon let out an impatient gasp. "But how can we prove anything? Offering to buy the ranch isn't admitting guilt." She shifted in her seat. "Besides, his name wasn't on the offer."

Jason said, "He could have a partner, or he could own that company."

"Or he could get a cut for persuading you to sell," Max added.

Jason had another idea. "That could be what that power of attorney nonsense was about."

"When he was here, he tried to get me to sign that, too," Sharon said.

Jason scowled. "If you had signed that paper, he could have sold the place without asking for your permission."

Max leaned forward. "I wouldn't have let her do that," he declared. "I was listening to that oily rascal from the kitchen."

"After all that courting, he wasn't interested in me at all," Sharon announced. "He wanted my inheritance."

"He could have planned to get it by marriage—as a last resort," Jason drawled. He slanted a look at her. "As handsome as he is, that may still be an option."

She sent him a scorching look, which his expression showed he thoroughly enjoyed.

Max said, "I've got it! I've got it!"

Jason and Sharon stared at him, waiting.

"We set up a trap," the little man went on. "We bait it with information about the Cattleman's Treasure and see who bites."

Jason looked doubtful. "There could be a lot of people biting on that one. It's been a rumor for a long time. Anyone could try to cash in on it."

"Not if we're smart about who we tell," Max insisted.

Jason wasn't buying it. "Once the word gets out, it's any man's game. We could have the whole town down on us."

"That could happen," Max admitted. He massaged his face. "I guess we'll have to think about it some more."

Jason slapped his knees. "Meanwhile, we need to go to town in the morning." He turned to Sharon. "Are you feeling strong enough for the trip? I could visit the preacher and undertaker for you."

"I'd like to go," she said. "I think I'll be fine, riding in the surrey." She stood. "If I'm going with you, I'd better say good night and get some rest."

The men said good night to her, but didn't move from their seats. Sharon heard the soothing sound of their husky voices droning on until she fell asleep.

&

When they set out for town after breakfast the next morning, Sharon scowled at the sky. "I'm beginning to hate the heat and the dust. If only there was some relief." Wedged between Jason and Max, she turned to Max. "Do you think the territory is going to end up like the Sahara? I've read *The Arabian Nights*, but I never wanted to live there."

"It's got to break sometime. Can't be much longer."

Jason let the reins hang loosely from his hands. "Corky and Wilson should be heading a bunch of cows toward the hills by this time. I hope the sheriff don't take it ill because they didn't come with us. We've got to get the herd moved. After we found the body, we didn't get a single thing done. Those beeves can't wait another day."

All around them the landscape was brown—the grass, the bushes, even the trees. They came to a stream that used to come up halfway to the buckboard's axle. It was completely dry, the streambed cracked and hard. The wagon jolted and rumbled across. The only things moving were several buzzards circling in the distance.

Sharon had nothing to report to the sheriff, so she went directly to the pastor's home, hoping that Rev. Nelson was there. His wife, a tiny, birdlike woman, let Sharon in.

"I came to see the pastor about funeral arrangements for my uncle," Sharon told her.

The woman's features showed concern. "He had a service at the ranch a few weeks ago," she said.

"We found his body yesterday," Sharon told her. "We want to bury him as soon as possible."

Trying unsuccessfully to hide her shock at the news, Mrs. Nelson's voice became soothing. "Of course. The pastor is in his study. He'll be glad to speak to you." She led the way through a narrow hall and opened the door. "Miss Hastings is here to see you, dear." She stood aside for Sharon to enter. "Would you like some coffee?"

"Water, please. We just drove from the ranch, and I'm thirsty. Thank you very much."

Leaving the door ajar, Mrs. Nelson scurried away.

The preacher rose to shake Sharon's hand. When she told him her errand, he frowned.

"It was foul play?" When Sharon nodded, he went on. "That's so hard to believe. Rudolph was a kind man, gruff at times but good deep down. I know of several people that he helped when they were in desperate straits."

Sharon came alert. "Would you mind telling me who they were?"

His face became pensive. "I'm not sure the parties involved would like it to be known."

"There's going to be a criminal investigation," she said urgently. "Since we can't seem to find any enemies, we were starting to think that someone he helped did this."

Steepling his fingers in front of his waistcoat, Rev. Nelson said, "There was the Widow Braddock and her four children. Rudolph found a buyer for their place, so they could move south to be near her relatives."

Sharon nodded. "I've heard about them. You know, he sold his share in the general store not long ago. I'm beginning to wonder if he didn't give away the money he made from that. There's no bank account, and nothing was recently paid on the mortgage."

"Right." He nodded. "Zach Ingles was another one. Fresh out of prison, no job, no money, and a family to feed. Rudolph took a chance on him, and it paid off. It's still paying off for Ingles."

"Was there anyone else?"

"He helped my wife and me numerous times. Fixed the roof on our house, brought us a milk cow, and a lot of other things, too many to list out." He smiled sadly. "The church is going to miss him." He drew in his lower lip, thinking. "There was a young fellow, a rascal that everyone considered a nuisance. Rudolph gave him a job, but the boy ended up stealing from him. This was three or four years back. Rudolph let him go, and we never heard from him again."

"His name?"

"Billy Gants. Wilson Gants' nephew."

seventeen

Forcing her mind back to the subject at hand, Sharon made arrangements for a funeral service at the church in two days. That should give the sheriff time to get what he needed from the doctor's examination.

Leaving the pastor and his wife shortly afterward, she hurried toward the sheriff's office and met Jason outside the door. She dove in before he could say anything. "Did you know about Uncle Rudolph firing Billy Gants?" she demanded.

He looked puzzled. "Of course. Billy and I practically grew up together."

"Do you think he may have come back for revenge?"

Taking her arm, Jason moved to a nearby bench in the shade. "Let's sit here. I can't take much more of that sun."

Staring at his face, Sharon wouldn't let her question die.

"Billy was trouble. There's no doubt about it," he told her. "I don't know if Wilson asked Rudolph to give Billy a job or not. One way or the other, Billy came to work with us. He only lasted about six months."

"He was caught stealing," she added.

He looked doubtful. "I wouldn't say that to anyone. Billy's got family here. Even if it were true, it would shame them, and they didn't do anything illegal."

Sharon glanced around. Five horses stood at the hitching rail in front of the general store, but no humans were in sight. She lowered her voice. "This is between us, Jason. I want to know if you think Billy could have come back for revenge."

Reluctantly, he said, "I suppose it's possible. From what his

151

sister says, Billy hasn't been to Farmington since Rudolph let him go. It's a grief to that family. It probably is to Billy, too. He can't see his family because of what he did."

At that moment Max stepped out of the sheriff's office and headed toward them in the rolling gait common to sailors and people who are both short and wide.

"Don't you think we should tell the sheriff?" Sharon demanded in a whisper before Max reached them.

"That's your call," he said, shrugging. "I can't make it for you. I personally don't think it's that important."

Irritated by his nonchalant attitude, she stood and marched into the sheriff's office. One of these days when he put her off like that, she'd forget everything Mrs. Minniver had worked so hard to teach her.

❧

Twenty minutes later, she stepped out and found Jason waiting for her on the same bench. He stood when he saw her.

"Max's at the general store," he told her. "We'll catch up to him."

"I haven't talked to the undertaker yet," she said primly.

"He's down at the end of the street." They paced six steps before Jason said, "So, what did the sheriff say?"

"He wrote it all down. That's all I know."

"Look, Sharon"—he tugged on her elbow, and she came around to face him—"I know you're anxious to get this behind us, but be careful. There are a lot of side issues in every question. Since you're new here, you could do a lot of damage without meaning to."

Finally, her shoulders relaxed and her chin came down. "I'm sorry, Jason. Patience has never been one of my virtues."

"Don't apologize," he said, his voice low. "It's understandable that you're upset. Just remember"—he leaned closer—"I'm on your side."

The undertaker's office was a small structure that resembled a smokehouse or a potting shed. Jason knocked and the undertaker, Darien Michaels, came to the door wearing a leather apron. His brand of cologne wouldn't have brought much on the open market. When he saw Jason and Sharon, his stoic expression never changed. "Good morning, Miss Hastings, Riordan."

"I just came from speaking to the preacher," Sharon said. "We'd like to have the funeral service the day after tomorrow at ten o'clock. Will that be convenient for you?"

He nodded once. "The doctor and I have already finished with Mr. Hastings. I'll build the coffin this afternoon." He paused. "Normally, the family brings clothes, but with the condition of the body it would be best to leave it as it is. We'll have a closed casket, of course."

Working hard at breathing as little as possible, Sharon gulped and said, "That will be fine, Mr. Michaels. Thank you."

As they walked away, Sharon turned to Jason and demanded, "Do you send him a quarter of a beef every spring, too? Or do I need to pay the man?"

Jason burst out laughing. He laughed until they reached the general store.

Max turned, a question in his eyes when they stepped inside the store. Still grinning, Jason stopped to look at the leather goods while Sharon went farther inside.

"Hello, Timothy," she said, smiling sweetly at the clerk.

"Sharon!" His face it up. "How are you doing? I've been wondering how the water hole is holding up."

Max glanced from Sharon to Timothy, then moved down the counter to look at a mound of cabbages piled on a table.

Timothy stepped closer. "How about another ride to Chimney Rock? I'm off tomorrow."

"I'd love to," Sharon said, "but we'd better wait at least two more weeks. I'm not completely back to full strength yet."

He came to stand directly across from her at the counter. "Have you been sick?" he asked.

She shook her head. "I had an accident, but I'm doing much better. When I'm ready, we'll go back up there. Believe me," she smiled broadly, "I'd go today if I could."

Jason stepped up. Glancing at him, Timothy hurried to wrap Max's purchases.

"Do you feel strong enough to stay around for a meal?" Jason asked her. "Or would you like me to fetch a box lunch from the restaurant and stop somewhere along the way for a picnic?"

Sharon sighed. "Max and I went to the restaurant the last time we were here. It was scorching hot and packed with people. I vote for a picnic."

"I second the motion," Jason said. "Since there are only three of us, the ayes have it." He called to Timothy, "Add five cans of peaches to that order, will you please?"

The clerk waved at him.

Jason looked down at Sharon. "I know a perfect spot in the shade where you can wait until we finish our business. You really ought to sit down and rest before we take off."

They strolled down the boardwalk to the stage station where a large awning blocked the sun from a smoothly carved bench with a sloping back and wide arms.

"There's no stage due for a couple of hours," he said. "You'll be comfortable here. I'll be back in a few minutes." With that, he hurried away.

Even with the shade, Sharon felt sticky and miserable. She thought about Billy Gants hiding in the trees or behind some rocks with a rifle.

Or maybe it wasn't Billy. Maybe it was some member of

the Gant family who was sore. One never could tell with situations like that.

On the ride home, the horses were anxious and leaning into the harness. "They're as miserable as we are," Jason commented as the wagon bounced down the trail. "Why not let them go? We can eat while we're riding."

"Hand me that box," Max groaned. "My belly button is about to kiss my backbone. I'm that hungry."

At that pace, the breeze cooled Sharon's burning face. She took off her bonnet and held it carefully in her lap.

Jason grinned at her. "Hand me a piece o' chicken" is all he said.

Wilson was waiting for them on the porch when they got back to the house. He came down the steps and grabbed the bridle. "Heinburg was just here. He said they're going to drive their herd to the northeast corner of our property. The water hole's dry. He said that O'Bannon doesn't want to, but his cattle are desperate."

Sharon gazed up at Jason.

He squeezed her hand. "There's enough water in that sector to last another couple of days. Meanwhile, we'll ride out that way and see how far up the main stream is dry. If it doesn't rain for a while yet, we may have to move our herd farther up into the mountains."

He spoke to Wilson. "Remind Corky that no one leaves the ranch yard without his sidearm and a rifle."

"Guns?" Sharon gasped. Her hands trembled as she grasped Jason's shoulders to step down from the buckboard. When she reached the ground, Wilson led the horses toward the barn, and Max headed into the house.

"It's going to be all right," he murmured, gazing into her eyes. "You'd better get some rest now. I'll take care of things, so don't worry."

"But what if someone comes here while you're gone? We still don't know who wants me out of the way."

Turning toward the house, Jason said, "Let me show you something." He led the way into the house with Sharon close behind him. He lifted the shotgun from over the mantel and brought it to her. It had SHARPS engraved on its side.

"Have you ever used a gun?" he asked.

When she shook her head, he said, "You press this release here." He showed her a knob near the end of the barrel. "That allows it to open." He pressed on the ends of the weapon and it came apart as it bent in the center. "This one holds two cartridges. See, it's loaded." He snapped the ends together with one quick motion.

He swung the barrel toward the ceiling and a rolled-up paper flew out. It landed on the floor in front of the rocking chair.

"What is that?" Sharon asked, hurrying to pick it up. She unrolled it, and Jason came to see. "It looks like a page from a ledger." She scanned down the closely written columns. Pacing to the table, she tried to spread it out, but it kept rolling up. Jason held two corners, and she held two.

"What have you got there?" Max asked, joining them.

"It looks like a business ledger," Jason said. "But there's no name on it."

"Let's see what's listed," Sharon said, peering at the tiny writing. "What are they buying and selling?" She read out, "Twenty-five pounds cornmeal, a hundred pounds molasses"— her finger slid down the page—"two coffee grinders, one keg of nails, six cases of paper, a hundred fountain pens. . ."

"It's Ingles' store," Max announced. "I'd stake my new stove on it."

"Wait a minute," Jason said. "What's so special about this page? Why was it hidden in the shotgun?" He pulled out a chair to sit down. Sharon and Max did the same.

"Read those off again, Sharon," Max said, "slower this time."

He closed his eyes, listening. Suddenly, he blinked and said to Jason, "Did you ever hear of Ingles selling paper and pens?"

Jason shook his head. "Old Starky at the newspaper office sells that kind of stuff. I asked about some when Lucy was still in school. Ingles said he wouldn't give the old man any competition because Mrs. Starky was so sick and he needed the money."

"I've heard about this kind of thing," Sharon said. "Sometimes when people want to cover up for missing money, they list purchases that never happened. It's called embezzling," she said, still staring at the page. "And the dates are shortly before Uncle Rudolph disappeared."

Max massaged his face. "You think that's why Rudolph sold out to Ingles?"

"Why would he sell out if the other man was wrong?" Jason asked. "Why not force Ingles to give up his half and take it all?" He stood. "Put that paper somewhere safe," he told Sharon. "I'm going to ride back into town and face Ingles."

She grabbed his sleeve. "Tell the sheriff," she said, coming to her feet. "Let him take care of it."

Jason's face was rigid. She held on to him, determined that he would listen. Finally, he relaxed. "You're right. I'll get the sheriff." He backed away. "But I've got to do it right away." He strode to the door. "With a fresh horse, I should be back in just a few hours." With a lingering look at her, he turned and rushed out.

Sharon rolled the paper into a tiny tube. "Where should I put it?" she asked Max.

"We might need the shotgun," he said. "Don't put it back in the barrel."

Moving slowly, she walked to the back door, looking all around to find a hiding place. She kept going down the steps and looked around the lean-to kitchen.

Sophie came to the fence and bawled for her. Sharon forgot about the page in her hands and hurried to pet her. "Sophie! You didn't forget me, did you, baby?"

Looking up, she spotted a crack in a beam under the roof of the goat's hut. It was a perfect fit. She slid the roll of paper into the crack and it loosened enough to fill the spot, invisible under the tin covering.

She drew the milking stool close to the fence and sat down. "Sophie, girl. You've grown so big."

eighteen

When Jason reached Farmington, the sheriff was already at home for the evening. He listened to Jason's story, then reached for his Stetson and went with him to the Ingles' home next to the store.

With a sinking feeling in his stomach, Jason stood to the side as Sheriff Feingold rapped on the door.

Timothy was the one to open it. "What can I do for you, Sheriff?" the young man asked, opening the door wider. "Would you like to come in? We're closed, but if you need something—"

"We're here to see your pa," Feingold said.

"He's in Albuquerque on a buying trip. He left yesterday, and he won't be back until later this week." He turned to Jason, puzzled. "Is there something I can do for you?"

"We'll wait until he gets back," the sheriff said. "Good evening."

Timothy nodded, said, "Good evening," and closed the door.

Jason and the sheriff returned to the street.

"I'll check on Zach when he gets back to town," Feingold said, shifting a toothpick in his teeth.

"Thanks, Sheriff. Much obliged." With no further conversation, Jason climbed into the saddle and turned the horse toward home. Let the law take care of things. He had a drought to worry about.

⁂

Sharon was dressed and ready to go before breakfast the next morning.

When Jason saw Sharon in the living room, his eyes narrowed. "Where are you going?" he asked.

She looked him straight in the eyes. "I'm going with you."

"Sharon. . ." His mouth set into a firm line.

"I'll be all right," she insisted. "It's better for me to be out there with you than to stay here and worry myself into a frazzled knot by the time you get back. If I get tired, I'll find a tree and take a break in the shade." She touched his arm. "Please, Jason."

He traced her face with his eyes, and his expression grew tender. "What if we end up camping on the range, or what if there's a problem with the Double O hands?" He lifted his hands as though to rest them on her shoulders, then dropped them to his sides. "I—we almost lost you once. I don't want to take any chances on a second time."

"It's so much cooler in the foothills," she said. "This heat is unbearable. Think of what it will be like for me if I stay here."

Wilson came in at that point, and Sharon moved into the dining area to sit at the table. Jason sat across the corner from her.

"I'd like to come along this time," Max said.

"Good idea," Jason replied. "Corky and Wilson could use an extra man."

When the meal was over, Sharon simply walked out of the house with the men. Wilson saddled Ginger, and they set off. If they spotted any stray Lazy H cattle along the way, the men would gather them up and push them north.

The sun was directly overhead when they crossed the fence line at the northern boundary of the Lazy H. The streambed was parched and dry as far as they could see.

"We may have to go up a ways before the water starts," Jason said, riding near Sharon. He peered at her face. "Are you feeling all right? Do you need to stop for a while?"

"I'm fine," she said. "I'm not anxious to stop in this heat. Let's get up where the temperature drops a little. Then I'll rest."

They spread out with Corky, Max, and Wilson far afield. Sharon followed the dry streambed with Jason fifty feet behind her. They rode that way for the better part of an hour. In the distance, the mountains stretched toward the sky. They seemed so close, but they were actually miles away.

Another two hours passed, and still not a trickle came down the depression that had once been rushing with water.

"I'm getting really thirsty," Sharon said when Jason rode up beside her. "I can imagine Ginger feels the same way." She took a long drink from her canteen and slid down to the ground. Wetting her bandanna, she swabbed out Ginger's nose and poured some water on the horse's long tongue. "Sorry, girl. That's the best I can do for now."

"I can't understand it," Jason said. "It was this dry back in '86, and we never lost the water hole."

"Maybe it's because of O'Bannon's cattle coming onto our land," Sharon said. "Twice as many cows. Or maybe more depending on how many Rudolph had back then."

Suddenly, a whistle reached them. One of the men waved his hat.

Jason said, "Looks like they've found something." He urged his gelding to a trot. After Sharon remounted Ginger, the horse took off running. Sharon let her go. There had to be water up ahead.

When they reached the hands, Corky said, "Some crazy hombre dammed up the stream. Look there!"

A pile of stones, sawed-off tree limbs, and dirt filled the streambed. Moving beyond it, Sharon drew up, shocked to see a wide, cool pond filled with clear water. "Who would do such a criminal thing?" she cried. "Why?"

Ginger walked into the center of the pond for a long drink.

Sharon pulled off her shoes and tied them together to hang them from the pommel and looped the strings of her bonnet over it as well. Laughing, she slid off the horse and into four feet of water. She let herself sink until the cooling liquid met her chin. "This is like heaven!" she cried. "Come on in!"

"I thought you hated to be wet!" Jason said, laughing at her.

"Do I?" she replied, scooping a handful of water at him. "That must have been some other girl."

Four pairs of boots hit the dust; four gun belts soon followed. Then the pond was filled with fully clothed people. They soaked and splashed and laughed and joked.

An hour passed before Jason said, "We've got to blast that blockade out of there."

Looking like a rain-soaked puppy, Wilson nodded. "I've got some shotgun cartridges. We can take the powder from them and make a big enough bang to blow out a hole. The water will do the rest."

Sharon was the last one out of the water. She plodded to the bank, dragging Ginger's reins behind her, and spent the next ten minutes wringing out her split skirt. Surprisingly, she felt good. She'd expected to be miserable in wet clothes, but she only felt cool.

Wilson shouted, "Everybody, get back! Way back!"

Sharon guided Ginger a hundred yards up the stream. She found a shady spot nearby to stretch out on the grass.

She took her cotton bonnet, folded it flat, and laid it under her head, then closed her eyes.

Suddenly, someone grabbed her arms and hauled her to her feet.

She screamed and thrashed around, but his strong fingers dug into her flesh, bruising her. "Settle down, Sharon," he snarled into her ear. "You'll only hurt yourself doing that."

She immediately froze. "Timothy!" she gasped. "What are you doing?"

"I'm saving my life," he said, dragging her downstream.

"No! They're going to blast the dam! We can't go down there."

His voice was harsh. "That's exactly why we're going there. Now stop struggling. I don't want to hit you, but I will if I have to."

Trembling, she decided to bide her time and do what he asked.

"Put your hands behind your back," he said. When she did, he tied her hands together and used her elbow as a handhold to drag her closer to the men. A few yards later, they stopped behind a large cottonwood tree at the very edge of the pond. Timothy pulled out his revolver.

"Riordan!" he shouted. "Stop!" He shot into the air. "Stop! If you blast that dam, Sharon's dead. Do you hear me? Dead!"

Think, Sharon, she told herself. *Stop panicking and think.* She watched her captor and marveled at the change in him. His face was grim, his eyes hard. He seemed like a totally different person from the smiling young man she thought she knew.

"Who is that?" Jason's voice boomed. "What do you want?"

"Stop trying to blast the dam, or I'll blast Sharon. And this time I'll finish the job!"

"Why are you doing this?" she asked Timothy. "What do you want from me?"

He grinned in her direction. His chilling smile stopped her breath. "I used to want you to leave Farmington," he said. "I wanted you to sell the ranch and leave." His smile faded. "I tried to make things so tough you'd give up ranching and no one would question it or blame you. Thirsty cattle, trouble with the neighbors, you name it. But you're too stubborn for that." He glanced in the direction of the ranch.

Sharon followed Timothy's line of sight. A pillar of black smoke rose into the sky and billowed out like a giant storm cloud.

"My house!" She let out a sob. "Timothy, why?"

"Evidence," he said. "You've got it, and I couldn't find it. One way or the other, it'll be gone now. Even if your men took off running, by the time they get home, it'll be too late. Everything's dry as tinder."

Peering around the tree, he went on, "Your uncle tore a page from the store ledger. He said it was to keep me honest. Actually, it was to hold me hostage. I had to watch every move I made for fear he'd turn me in."

"You were stealing from your own father?"

He glared at her. "He never paid me a dime. All I took was my rightful wages. That's all I took." He peeked around the tree. "Rudolph said he'd give me a second chance. Every six months he checked out the books to make sure they were all right." Holding his pistol high, he glanced at her. "I took it as long as I could. Then I knew I had to get rid of him."

She felt a weight on her chest that made it hard to breathe. He was talking too much. He had no intention of letting her go.

She tried to look around the tree. Where was Jason? Why hadn't he answered?

Ingles yanked her back. "Stay right there, missy," he ground out. "I'm not playing around, you hear me? You'll get yourself killed."

"How can you imagine you'll get away with this?" she demanded. "Someone will know what you've done. You'll go to prison."

He shook his head. "O'Bannon is going to take the blame for this one. At least his ranch hands will. Everybody in town knows how desperate the Double O is for water. They know crossing a fence line means trouble between ranchers."

"Ingles!" Jason boomed from close behind them. A shot split the air.

Timothy jerked around.

Sharon lowered her shoulder and hit him under the rib cage with all the force she could muster. He lost his balance and tumbled into the pond.

Jason and Wilson plunged into the water and overcame him before he could come up for air.

"The house!" Sharon screamed. "He's burning down the house!"

Tossing his head to fling his wet hair from his eyes, Jason called, "We saw the smoke a few minutes ago! Max's already headed for home!"

Corky arrived and cut the ropes to set Sharon free as Wilson tied Timothy hand and foot with rawhide pigging strings. A nonstop string of profanity spewed from the young man until Jason pulled out a handkerchief and stuffed it into Timothy's mouth.

"He was stealing from his father," Sharon said. "Uncle Rudolph tore out that ledger page to keep him honest, so Timothy killed him."

Jason said, "Corky, take this *outlaw* to the sheriff. Sharon and I will go to town later and tell him what we know." Looking at Sharon, his mouth quirked in. "We lost the evidence," he said. "That's not good."

"No, we didn't. I hid it in the nanny pen," Sharon replied with a glint in her eye. "Did you hear that, Timothy?"

He mumbled something around the cloth in his mouth and glared at her. Corky yanked him toward the horses.

Wilson said, "You folks had better stand back. I'm going to blast that dam before anything else happens." He trudged away.

Hiking upstream, Jason and Sharon stopped in the middle of a grove of trees. Shaking so badly that she could hardly stand, Sharon said, "What am I going to do? The house is gone. Where am I going to live?"

Jason drew her into his arms and held her until her sobs subsided.

A deep, rumbling *boom* shook the ground beneath them. Sharon cringed and he drew her close again.

In a few minutes, he said, "We'd better check on Wilson. I don't like leaving a man when there's a dangerous job like this. Then we'll head back to the ranch yard."

He whistled and got an answering, "Yeah! I'm all right!"

The explosion had indeed blasted a gap in the dam. Water gushed out, carrying sticks and debris with it. The three of them stood on the banks, watching as the hole widened and the sides of the dam caved in.

"That's good enough for now," Jason said. "We'll come back later and clean it out."

Wilson nodded. "I wonder how much that will affect the water hole," he said. "Should be at least eight or ten inches."

"Enough to get us through until it rains," Jason agreed.

"How despicable to stop up the water when it's so low!" Sharon exclaimed. "And he seemed so nice."

Jason helped her mount Ginger, and she immediately set off for home. A few minutes later, Jason and Wilson caught up with her. No one talked on the ride home. The black cloud had thinned out across the horizon. Not much smoke was rising from the ground now.

When they reached the yard, there were twenty men in a bucket brigade leading from the horse trough to the house. At first glance, it appeared that the fire had started at the front porch, now a charred and smoking skeleton. The roof was burnt halfway up the front, but no flames were visible.

Max waved and stepped out of the line to meet them. His clothes and face were black. Only his eyes showed white around the edges. "O'Bannon's men saw the first smoke and came a-running," he said. "They were too late to save the porch or the living room, but the rest of the house is intact." He smeared more soot over his cheeks as he massaged his jaw. "But the smoke. . ." He turned toward Sharon. "I'm afraid everything inside that was cloth or paper is ruined, honey. I'm so sorry."

Sharon stared at the smoldering house, numb from her eyes to her toes. Jason came to help her down. She slid into his waiting arms and hid her face in his shirt.

"Where can I go?" she asked.

"You're not going anywhere," he murmured. "You're going to stay here with me."

"But the house—"

"Is only boards and windows," he finished. He put his arm around her and led her toward the barn. "Let's get you out of the sun," he said. "You're all in."

They sat on the bench outside in the shade, watching the flurry of activity like spectators at a horse race. "Why don't you sell half of the land?" Jason asked her.

"What? Give up now?"

"Not all of it. Sell the lower half to O'Bannon, from the water hole south. That would give him the water he needs, and you could build a house on the north side where it isn't so hot and dry. We could dig out a new water hole where the small stream forks off the big one. It would be perfect for cattle, much better than here. As things are now, we don't use a third of the land we can lay claim to."

She considered that. "You may have something there."

"He may give you five thousand for half of it, and consider it a bargain," Jason went on. "It'll make all the difference to him, Sharon. I don't see how he could refuse. Then you could pay off the mortgage and have plenty left to build a nice house."

"But where will I live in the meantime?"

"Lucy and Ma will be delighted to have you." He stood. "Come here." Taking her hand, he led her into the barn. When they reached the comforting dimness inside, he pulled her into his arms like he'd never let her go. "I love you, Sharon," he whispered. "I want you to marry me."

"How could you?" she asked. "I'm stubborn and opinionated. I've ignored your advice and—"

He stilled her lips with a warm and tender kiss that came from deep within. When he finally released her, he murmured into her hair, "You're feisty and funny and as beautiful as the morning sun."

"I love you, Jason," she said and he kissed her again.

Entwined in his arms, Sharon forgot about the ruined house. She forgot about the hardships and sorrows of that endless summer. Sharon had just come home.

epilogue

On the second day of September, the Riordan cabin glowed from the stones on the fireplace to the windows on the porch. Platters stacked high with flaky pastries and tiny pies covered every surface in the kitchen. Max had an apron over his white shirt and black tie. He was wiping counters and cabinet fronts while Mrs. Riordan sat at the table, happily talking of her girlhood days and the winsome ways of her only beau, a handsome man named Daniel Riordan.

In the back bedroom, Sharon giggled. "I can't believe it, Lucy! I can't believe it's today. My wedding day!"

Beaming, Lucy hugged her, then gently pushed Sharon into a chair. "If you don't sit still, how can I finish your hair?"

Sharon patted Lucy's hand. "I'm glad you're going to be my sister, Lucy girl."

"Going to be?" she asked around pins in her mouth. "I already am, you goose."

"Who would have ever dreamed when I gave you that trunk full of clothes that I'd have to take some of them back?"

"If you weren't so generous, you would have lost *everything*." Lucy hugged her from behind. "Except Jason. You could have never lost him."

Sharon's smile was dazzling.

The front yard had been swept clean. Pots of flowers lined a wide aisle between two banks of benches. At the front stood more flowers and Rev. Nelson in his black suit, reading his notes for the service.

The ceremony began at noon. Jason stood before the

preacher as Mrs. Nelson sang "O Promise Me" and Lucy strolled down the aisle. Then Sharon stepped out holding Max's arm and pacing toward the man she loved.

" 'Marriage is an institution of divine appointment,'" the pastor read from his little black book. " 'It is the most important step in life and should not, therefore, be entered into lightly, but soberly and discreetly.'" A few minutes later, he said, "Sharon, do you take this man to be your lawful husband. . . ?"

Gazing into Jason's eyes, she said, "I do."

Soon after, Jason also said, "I do."

A deep rumbling from overhead drowned out the pastor's next words. A second rumble sounded when he said, "You may kiss your bride."

As Jason lifted Sharon's veil, she melted into his arms while the first fat raindrops fell. As he pulled her to him, the sky opened up.

Gasps went up from the guests. Benches overturned as they raced for the shelter of the porch.

Jason lifted his head to say, "You're getting wet, Mrs. Riordan."

She laughed aloud and leaned her face back to catch the spray on her cheeks. "Yes!" She closed her eyes, savoring the coolness. And he kissed her again.

A Letter To Our Readers

Dear Reader:

In order that we might better contribute to your reading enjoyment, we would appreciate your taking a few minutes to respond to the following questions. We welcome your comments and read each form and letter we receive. When completed, please return to the following:

Fiction Editor
Heartsong Presents
PO Box 719
Uhrichsville, Ohio 44683

1. Did you enjoy reading *Sharon Takes a Hand* by Rosey Dow?
   ❑ Very much! I would like to see more books by this author!
   ❑ Moderately. I would have enjoyed it more if

   _____

   _____

   _____

2. Are you a member of **Heartsong Presents**? ❑ Yes ❑ No
   If no, where did you purchase this book? _____

   _____

3. How would you rate, on a scale from 1 (poor) to 5 (superior), the cover design? _____

4. On a scale from 1 (poor) to 10 (superior), please rate the following elements.

   ____ Heroine   ____ Plot
   ____ Hero   ____ Inspirational theme
   ____ Setting   ____ Secondary characters

5. These characters were special because? _____
_____
_____

6. How has this book inspired your life? _____
_____
_____

7. What settings would you like to see covered in future
   Heartsong Presents books? _____
_____
_____

8. What are some inspirational themes you would like to see
   treated in future books? _____
_____
_____

9. Would you be interested in reading other **Heartsong
   Presents** titles?   ❏ Yes   ❏ No

10. Please check your age range:
     ❏ Under 18   ❏ 18-24
     ❏ 25-34   ❏ 35-45
     ❏ 46-55   ❏ Over 55

Name _____
Occupation _____
Address _____
City, State, Zip_____

Hearts♥ng

HEARTSONG PRESENTS TITLES AVAILABLE NOW:

(If ordering from this page, please remember to include it with the order form.)

Presents

Great Inspirational Romance at a Great Price!

Heartsong Presents books are inspirational romances in contemporary and historical settings, designed to give you an enjoyable, spirit-lifting reading experience. You can choose wonderfully written titles from some of today's best authors like Wanda E. Brunstetter, Mary Connealy, Susan Page Davis, Cathy Marie Hake, Joyce Livingston, and many others.

When ordering quantities less than twelve, above titles are $2.97 each.
Not all titles may be available at time of order.

Visit ReaderService.com Today!

As a valued member of the Harlequin Reader Service, you'll find these benefits and more at ReaderService.com:

- Try 2 free books from any series
- Access risk-free special offers
- View your account history & manage payments
- Browse the latest Bonus Bucks catalog

Don't miss out!

If you want to stay up-to-date on the latest at the Harlequin Reader Service and enjoy more content, make sure you've signed up for our monthly News & Notes email newsletter. Sign up online at ReaderService.com or by calling Customer Service at 1-800-873-8635.

HARLEQUIN SELECTS COLLECTION

19 FREE BOOKS IN ALL!

From Robyn Carr to RaeAnne Thayne to Linda Lael Miller and Sherryl Woods we promise (actually, GUARANTEE!) each author in the Harlequin Selects collection has seen their name on the *New York Times* or *USA TODAY* bestseller lists!

don't have to rush into anything. Thea has the network she needs to be safe now and the future will always be a question mark, so I can take my time. Vanessa. Steve. You. Reyna. Sean. Your father. You're a part of that foundation I want for me and for Thea. If falling in love takes a while, I'm okay."

Was he saying this correctly? He wanted Brisa. He'd prove they worked with enough time. He waited for her answer.

"No rush. I'm glad. But what if I've set you up with the right woman this time?" Brisa beamed. "What if falling in love only takes a minute? You okay with that?"

His smile grew. "Even better."

* * * * *

If you missed Reyna and Sean's romance,
The Dalmatian Dilemma,
*and for other great novels in
the Veterans' Road miniseries,
visit Harlequin Heartwarming at
www.Harlequin.com today!*